DOC

THE STONES OF BLOOD

DOCTOR WHO

THE STONES OF BLOOD

Based on the BBC television serial
The Stones of Blood by David Fisher

DAVID FISHER

1

BBC Books, an imprint of Ebury Publishing
20 Vauxhall Bridge Road,
London SW1V 2SA

BBC Books is part of the Penguin Random House group of companies whose addresses can be found at global.penguinrandomhouse.com

Doctor Who is a BBC Wales production for BBC One

Executive producers: Chris Chibnall and Matt Strevens

Audio edition first published by AudioGO Ltd, 2011

First published by BBC Books in 2022

www.penguin.co.uk

A CIP catalogue record for this book is available from the British Library

ISBN 9781785947940

Editorial director: Albert DePetrillo
Project editor: Steve Cole
Audio edition project editor: Michael Stevens
Cover design: Two Associates
Cover illustration: Anthony Dry

Printed and bound in Great Britain by Clays Ltd, Elcograf S.p.A.

The authorised representative in the EEA is Penguin Random House Ireland, Morrison Chambers, 32 Nassau Street, Dublin D02 YH68

Penguin Random House is committed to a sustainable future for our business, our readers and our planet. This book is made from Forest Stewardship Council® certified paper.

Contents

Foreword

Nick Fisher

'Writing is like a muscle,' David Fisher would say. 'If you don't exercise that muscle, it gets flabby.'

My dad was a writer to his core. Stamped all the way through him, like a stick of rock. A writer and a reader. He was perpetually surrounded by piles of books. One of his favourite places to read was in the bath, during the day, sometimes smoking a cigar. He was unspeakably well-read, everything from the classics and historical novels to crime thrillers. He loved a crime thriller. And he had a soft spot for science fiction too.

On the other hand, I wasn't a willing young reader. Even though he read to me and my sisters most nights when we were young (he was a big Dr Seuss fan), the love for the written word wasn't obvious in my own DNA. I resisted any sort of study or reading until I was 13 when, under threat of being expelled from grammar school, my parents effectively grounded me for the summer and my dad bought me a copy of Ray Bradbury's *The Golden Apples of the Sun*. I was so bored by my incarceration, I gobbled it up. So he followed it with copies of *Something Wicked This Way Comes*, *A Clockwork Orange*, *Catch-22* and finally *Slaughterhouse 5*. This was my introduction to Dad's taste in literature, not the Dickens and Shakespeare that I struggled to consume at school.

My dad found it strange and a little uncomfortable that he became most famous for his episodes of *Doctor Who*. He wrote so many different things during his life, many totally created by him, whereas he said he sometimes felt like a gun for hire on *Doctor Who*. Because he was writing for a lead character who had been created by another writer, he viewed his scripts as somehow slightly removed. He was, as he put it, 'playing with someone else's toys'. And yet there is so much of the real David Fisher – his interests and passions – in stories like *The Stones of Blood*.

Like some forms of exercise, writing can be painful. TV writing especially can be fraught with reconfigured storylines, budget and location restrictions, actors of varying abilities, rewrites, redrafts, cuts and sometimes excruciatingly painful edits. David never found it easy – no one does – and he often yearned for another form of writing that would seem more free, more authored, more *him*.

And so he tried everything. In his career, he was a very successful cartoonist, a children's book author and illustrator, a journalist, and the lyricist for at least three musicals, one of which was produced and performed at the Cockpit theatre. He tried his hand at crime thrillers and wrote several heavily researched non-fiction books about espionage and the Second World War, as well as making a documentary about the early days of unpowered aircraft.

He loved to research. He was often at his happiest when he was travelling to Germany or France to spend two weeks digging through dusty archives and interviewing ancient veterans during the day and consuming snails and gallons of red wine at night.

David was a man of many passions: cooking, eating and drinking were three of his favourites, which he would pursue with the creativity and zeal that he brought to his writing. When I was five and we lived in central Glasgow, he made his own gnocchi. No one had even heard of gnocchi in Glasgow in 1966, let alone made it! He made his own wine out of home-grown parsnips. He brewed beer and cultivated vegetables like spaghetti marrows and celeriac.

Dad loved to hunt, too – for stories, for knowledge, ideas, flavours, sensations and experiences. He often said that the bit of writing he enjoyed most of all was the research; a constant regret of his was that he'd never attended university. He'd never been able to indulge himself in study. He claimed he'd been offered a place at Oxford University, but was unable to take it up because his father had no money, and instead David had to go out to work.

I've never been entirely convinced of this version of events, but my dad never let facts get in the way of a good story. And if he wasn't writing one, what he enjoyed instead was to tell one. Preferably with a glass in his hand that was being regularly refilled.

Part of his regret about not attending university was that he thought he would have made a good don; a learned professor type, who could talk about literature all day long and enjoy big boozy lunches in the refectory whilst entertaining his peers and students. And maybe he would've. Maybe David Fisher *should* have been a literary professor. But then he never would have written all those cracking TV episodes, stories that have entertained millions rather than just a few academics.

Not going to university made him feel intellectually insecure at times, as though he'd missed out on some rite of passage that would have made him seem more genuinely clever. As though he needed a degree; a certificate to prove his intellect. As a result of not going to university himself, he was very keen that my sisters and I should all have the opportunity to go. Sadly, I wasn't a natural academic.

Although writing was his life, it was at times a painful cross to bear, and he told me from a very early age: 'Whatever you do, don't become a writer . . . It's a terrible business.'

I did, of course.

Thirty-eight years of professional writing later, I agree with my dad, to a degree. It is not without a certain amount of discomfort. But at least neither of us ever had to hold down a proper job.

David definitely would have hated that.

Chapter I

The Tor

About four thousand years ago there was nothing remarkable about the place. It was an ordinary West Country tor, not far from the sea. It was covered with skimpy grass, brambles, briars and a few stunted bushes. There was a scattering of small stones on the ground, detritus from the retreat of the glacier of the last Ice Age.

For centuries herders had grazed their meagre flocks of sheep and goats and scrawny cattle nearby. Hunters had hunted game there, though there was never enough feed to attract the larger species. Only rabbits had made Bodcombe Tor their own, and even then not in great numbers. All in all, it was a very ordinary place.

Then one day something strange happened. A momentary tremor, in the blink of an eye. A sense of slippage. An infinitesimal movement barely noticeable to anyone, as if the whole landscape had fractionally shifted . . .

From then on the place imperceptibly changed. The rabbits vanished. The hunters and herdsmen began to give the place a wide berth. No one went there any more. Bodcombe Tor had become a place of ill omen.

But then a young local shaman had a vision. A series of visions, in fact. He had had that sort of thing before, of course – he was a shaman, after all. Visions were his stock in trade. Yet in the past these had been little more than fleeting glimpses of the past or the future, often confusing, occasionally illuminating, essentially benign. What he was experiencing now was something of an entirely different order. These visions were clear, peremptory, more like commands than intimations of a world ruled by mysterious unseen forces. This clarity and force soon became frightening.

In a series of dreams, the shaman encountered a strange woman, who told him she was a goddess and must be worshipped. Moreover, she must be obeyed. This tor, she declared, this small, bleak hilltop, had now become a holy place, sacred to her. Whether he liked it or not, he had become her servant, and as such must obey her every command. Failure to do so would invoke the full fury of her wrath.

At first the shaman doubted the significance of this new revelation. He knew that not all visions were benign or even sensible. Indeed, there were false visions which could lead to disaster, destroying both the visionary and believer. It behoved him, therefore, to be cautious. Respectful but cautious. What did the Goddess want of him?

Blood, came the answer.

Sacrifices. Children or adults; age and gender were immaterial. The Goddess demanded blood. Human blood.

At this the shaman took fright. He was not unused to the idea of human sacrifices, and in the past had himself cut the throat of the odd prisoner of war. But that had been a gesture of gratitude from the community to the tribal gods for bringing a victory or a good harvest. Quid pro quo. This Goddess was clearly very different from the familiar tribal deities. Who knew where fulfilling her wishes might lead?

The shaman prevaricated, tried to put the Goddess out of his mind. He avoided Bodcombe Tor, her holy place, for days on end. All in vain. Every night he dreamed of great birds swooping down, attacking him, and he would wake up screaming, bathed in sweat. The Goddess clearly had no intention of letting him go.

In the end it was fear and desperation which drove him back to the tor to try and plead with the Goddess. Perhaps she would show mercy in her own sacred place.

But when he reached the tor, he found the most astonishing sight. The place was covered with birds. Hundreds of them. Blackbirds, crows, finches, ravens, thrushes, choughs, gulls from the nearby coast – birds of every size and shape. They arose in a flock as he approached and began flying round his head, calling and screeching. He turned to flee. But then the Goddess spoke to him.

'Do not be afraid,' she said. Her words echoed strangely inside his head. 'There is nothing to be afraid of. The birds are my messengers and do my bidding. You are quite safe as long as you obey me. Do you understand?'

The shaman *didn't* understand, but he nodded. He simply wanted to escape, though he doubted that she would allow him to do so. He fell to his knees. At this sign of submission suddenly the birds attacked him. The crows went for his face and plucked out his eyes. The pain was indescribable. He screamed in agony.

'Blindness is nothing,' whispered the Goddess. 'Now you will be able to see through my eyes. It will help you to become my perfect servant.'

He was still on his knees, his face covered in blood and still screaming, when some herdsmen found him. They helped him back to his cave and one tried to treat his wounds. The shaman shook him off and screamed that they should leave him.

Then the shaman lay alone and still in the dark. His eyes were gone; his world should've been black as night. And yet still shadows shifted in the pits behind his eyelids. Crimson shadows.

In the years that followed, worshippers built a temple for the Goddess of Bodcombe Tor. Nothing as complex as Stonehenge or Carnac. After all, they were a small tribe with only a blind shaman to guide them. What the Goddess required, it seemed, was a symbol indicating that she resided in that place.

So six huge monoliths were erected and arranged in a half circle, with an altar stone in the centre. Mysteriously, three more stones were said to appear when blood sacrifices were made. Then the six stones became nine. And what was truly miraculous, people said, was that when the blood was poured over them it was immediately absorbed.

You could see the stones drink blood!

As years turned to centuries, the stories grew stranger, darker. The legend of the Nine Dancers of Bodcombe Tor was passed down through the generations. These dancers had all been invited to a party, so the story went, but three of them arrived late – by which time the food and drink had been consumed and the dancing come to an end. So, feeling thirsty after their long journey, the three latecomers drank the blood of the six sleeping revellers and danced all night.

In yet another version of the tale, the stones were christened the Nine Travellers because periodically three of them went walkabout, though no one knew where they went or why. Another, more sinister, tale was that if there had been no blood sacrifices for any length of time, then the stones grew thirsty and went off hunting on their own account. And woe betide whomever they met.

Over millennia, the myths and misadventures

weaved and wobbled into a fine old mishmash of West Country folklore and provided a field day for local antiquarians and anthropologists. As a result, numerous learned papers were written about Bodcombe Tor, and it became the occasion for scholarly internecine warfare between experts in which no quarter was asked for or given.

In 1705, for example, the Rev. Cassius Pinchpenny, rector of Bodcombe Church, published a paper in which he identified the Goddess with the harpies of classical mythology. A view which was immediately rubbished by Dr Sheerwater, Dean of St Botolph's, who identified her as belonging to Teutonic myths. Another reverent gentleman opined that she was of Viking origin. And so on.

The truth was that Bodcombe Moor had become a perfect breeding ground for legends. Nearby the Stones stood Bodcombe Manor, built in 1672 by the elderly Lord George Montcalm at the behest of his new wife, a gypsy woman who was believed to have been a witch. Montcalm and the three children by his first wife died of the plague in spite of the fact that, strangely, no other cases were reported in the area that year.

The new Lady Montcalm went from strength to strength, or more correctly from death to death. She married three more times – each husband surviving only long enough to make a will in her favour. A score of lovers also came to a grisly end, some being found exsanguinated in the middle of the stone circle. Though she was popular with the local gentry, who enjoyed both her favours and her hospitality in abundance, the increasing body count could not be ignored for ever. When a local magistrate, one of her few surviving lovers, indicated that he was going to arrest her for witchcraft and/or murder, the lady vanished. She was said to have thrown herself over the cliffs of Bodcombe Bay. But her body was never discovered. Nevertheless the legend of the wicked Lady Montcalm survived. Centuries later, several novels and at least two movies mined the story to good effect.

After the disappearance of Lady Montcalm, the manor remained in female hands for at least three-quarters of a century. Fortunately none of the new owners showed any inclinations towards the criminality of their infamous predecessor. They tended to be deeply respectable, if occasionally eccentric widow ladies. Indeed, Mrs Trefusis, who lived alone at the manor for over fifty years, came to be regarded as something of a Miss Havisham – dining alone in the Great Hall night after night. She saw no one. Entertained no one. Her only relaxation was to drive out to the Nine Travellers in her carriage. What she did in the ruins of the stone circle, no one knew. Some local boys claimed they had seen her dancing there. But this was clearly nonsense. Stories of death and disappearance on the moor persisted, but none was investigated with any consequence. It was just one of those places, people murmured darkly.

On the death of the reclusive Mrs Trefusis and her subsequent interment in the family crypt, a distant cousin inherited the manor. She was Senhora Camara, widow of a wealthy Brazilian. Unlike her cousin, she proved to be something of a local Lady Bountiful – paying for the construction of some alms houses for the indigent elderly in Bodcombe Parva and also for a new stained-glass window in St Olaf's church. This window, according to Pevsner, is very fine and represents St Francis feeding the birds, one of which appears to be a vulture. It is said to be the only representation of a vulture in stained glass anywhere in England. Senhora Camara was foreign, of course, and known to be a great bird lover.

In later years the female influence upon the manor waned, as did the line of family inheritance. The hall and its land was leased to a variety of landlords, notable amongst which was one Anton de Vries, a gentleman of Anglo-Indian descent who became an active member of the local community in the late 1960s.

Sadly, as we will see, his notability derives mainly from one particular circumstance: the manner of his death.

Chapter II

Professor Rumford

Inside the TARDIS, the Doctor was engaged in something of a puzzle. He was struggling to fit two gleaming, translucent objects together, each one a segment of the powerful Key to Time. The segments were fabulous in appearance, radiating light in every direction from their multifaceted surface. These were two of the most precious artefacts in the universe, and four more still languished in the far corners of Time and Space, waiting to be located by the Doctor and his Time Lady assistant, Romana. Their mission to retrieve the Key to Time had so far brought them into great danger on the planets Ribos and Calufrax, and they both knew that probably far worse was yet to come.

For now, though, the Doctor had a more pressing task in hand: the unification of two segments to make one. It wasn't going well. The recently located second segment was supposed to fit into its appropriate niche on the first – but it didn't seem to want to go. Even when the Doctor hammered it with his shoe.

'Go in, blast you!' he shouted. But the segment refused to cooperate.

Alerted by the noise, Romana, an attractive female humanoid in the first flush of youth, entered the control room.

'Should you be doing that?' she asked, registering both the Doctor's expression and the upraised shoe.

'I'm trying to get it to fit together,' he growled.

Romana tut-tutted several times, and shook her head.

'I wish you wouldn't do that,' said the Doctor irritably. 'You sound like a defective outboard motor!'

Ignoring the obscure reference, Romana asked gently, 'Have you tried jiggling it – instead of brute force?'

'Jiggling it! That's hardly scientific language.'

She sighed. 'You know what I mean.'

The Doctor made a half-hearted show at trying yet again to unite the recalcitrant segments. 'There,' he said. 'I've jiggled it and it still won't fit.'

'Do you mind if I have a go?' she asked.

'If you think you can,' he replied dismissively.

Romana took the two segments, and within seconds had fitted them together quite easily.

The Doctor chose to appear scornful rather than impressed. 'Is that what they teach you now at the Academy on Gallifrey – jiggling?'

But before Romana could reply, the whole atmosphere in the control room changed. Lights dimmed. Dials on the multi-sided control console ceased to register. Even the temperature seemed to fall several degrees. Suddenly the whole room echoed to the sound of a deep, sepulchral voice. It sounded as if it came from some vast underground cavern.

'BEWARE THE BLACK GUARDIAN!' it boomed.

Romana shivered involuntarily. She did not scare easily, but finding that they were apparently no longer alone in the TARDIS came as a shock. 'What was that, Doctor? What does it mean?'

The Doctor's reply was sombre, as if he had recognised the timbre of the voice immediately. 'It means that we must continue with our mission and not waste time on puzzles. The sooner we arrive at our next destination and start looking for the third segment, the better.' With that he busied himself at the controls.

The Doctor's mission had been ordered by the White Guardian, one of the most powerful beings in the universe, otherwise known as the Guardian of Light in Time. His direct opposite was the Black Guardian, and they both sought the Key to Time. Ordinarily too powerful for any one being to control, the Key had been divided into six pieces and scattered throughout the universe, disguised through the power of transmutation, so that they would be safe. Now, though, at a time when the delicate balance of the universe was off-kilter, the White Guardian sought to use the reassembled Key to restore the natural balance of the universe. Meanwhile, the Black Guardian desired it to do the exact opposite, his sole aim being to plunge the entire cosmos into chaos. The Key, once fully assembled and activated, was the only thing capable of bringing all Time to a stop.

Romana had been assigned to the Doctor's mission as his assistant, much against his wishes. Already, though, something of a grudging friendship had grown up between them. To aid them in their quest, they had been given a wand-like device which they called the Tracer. When plugged into the TARDIS console, it would lead the time-and-space craft to the regions where each segment lurked. Then, when carried by the Doctor and Romana, the Tracer would lead them to a segment's precise location. Finally, when pressed to the object whose disguise the segment had taken, it would perform a reverse transmutation to reveal a glimmering, many-sided jewel.

As usual, the Doctor was also accompanied by his faithful robotic companion, K-9. Essentially, K-9 was a powerful automaton, designed in the appropriate shape of a terrestrial dog, the size of a terrier. His great advantage, as far as the Doctor was concerned, was that he didn't need feeding or watering or being taken for walks, and he lived quite happily in the TARDIS. Indeed, K-9 seemed almost to have acquired some of the characteristics of a real dog. Perhaps because the Doctor treated him like one.

'Sensors indicate TARDIS landing imminent, master,' K-9 now announced in his clipped mechanical tones.

'Thank you, K-9,' replied the Doctor. 'What would we do without you?' He checked the controls of the TARDIS and informed Romana, 'We're landing.'

Romana recalled both the snowy alleys of Ribos and the grim landscape of Calufrax and hoped for somewhere warmer this time. 'Where are we?'

The Doctor was grinning broadly as he declared, 'Earth!'

She smiled back ruefully. 'Your favourite planet.'

'How did you know that?'

'Before I left Gallifrey I was told that you visit the place at the slightest excuse. They also told me it's awkwardly placed on one of the arms of the galaxy, and there always seems to be trouble there.'

'Not always,' he said, rather hurt. 'Just sometimes. It's pretty civilised on the whole.'

Romana checked the instruments on the console. 'Oxygen level acceptable,' she read. 'And some kind of liquid precipitation is in progress.'

'Sometimes you sound just like K-9,' the Doctor observed. 'What you mean is it's raining outside. It often rains in England, which is where we happen to be. It's what they would describe here as a nice day.'

Romana was unconvinced. 'Ah yes, that's the other thing they said about Earth. It's wet.'

Rather taken aback by his assistant's lack of enthusiasm for his favourite planet, the Doctor pointed at her feet and said, 'I hope you're not planning on coming out in those silly shoes.'

Romana glanced down at the high-heeled slingback sandals she had found in the TARDIS wardrobe. She rather liked them, not least because they added height to her stature – never a bad thing when standing up to the Doctor. 'I am, actually,' she resolved. 'What's wrong with them?'

Now it was the Doctor's turn to tut. If she wouldn't be told, that was her look-out. 'Nothing, nothing,' he murmured. 'Be it on your own head – or even feet.' Then, keen to inject a little light-heartedness into the proceedings, he called out brightly, 'Anyone for tennis? I'm sure we've got a couple of rackets somewhere on board.'

This time Romana decided to ask about the reference rather than ignore it. 'Tennis?'

'It's an English expression. Translated it means, "Is anyone coming outdoors to get soaked?"'

Romana shook her head sadly; sometimes she wished the Doctor would be more serious. She removed the Tracer from its portal in the console and tucked it into her belt. Perhaps they would find segment number three quickly, then leave this damp planet and move on to somewhere more civilised where it didn't rain. 'Am I dressed appropriately?' she asked the Doctor, indicating the wide-skirted dress she had chosen to go with the shoes.

'For what?' he enquired. 'You look all right. At least you won't frighten the horses.' He put up his umbrella and stepped out into the English air. K-9 went to follow him, but the Doctor stopped the little robot in his tracks. 'Not now, K-9. Stay on guard. We don't yet know if these particular natives are friendly. If they are, I'll come and take you for a walk later.' Cheerily, he strode from the room.

Romana paused before following, to put a quick question to the robot dog. Her natural instinct was to learn new facts, not let them pass by unnoticed. And if she was to spend time on Earth, she ought to know as much as possible about its customs.

'K-9, what is tennis?'

'Real, lawn or table, mistress?'

Romana thought for a moment, and then finally gave up: life on this planet was clearly more complicated than she had imagined. 'Oh, forget it!' she said, and followed the Doctor out into the rain.

Literal as ever, K-9 obeyed his instructions to the letter. He erased all information about tennis – real, lawn and table – from his memory banks.

Outside, the Doctor and Romana were breathing damp English air and taking in the countryside. The TARDIS had landed on a moor with green hillsides and grass underfoot, and what looked like a village in the distance. Suddenly the sun came out, warming the heather and the two travellers.

'Pretty, isn't it?' said the Doctor, hoping to enthuse his companion with the West Country scenery.

But Romana was not to be cajoled. At the best of times her appetite for the great outdoors was limited, largely because she had experienced so little of it on Gallifrey. Her home planet was beautiful, but where she had lived most of her life was essentially urban. There were prairies and savannahs on Gallifrey, but she herself had never seen them: she had practically no experience of wide-open spaces. Her life had been spent almost exclusively indoors, where inclement weather was banned: the Academy, where she had spent much of her time, was regulated to be neither too hot nor too cold. There was no rain, no snow, no fog, no heat waves, just a pleasant, warm, ambient temperature at all times. Time Lords were not encouraged to seek out climatic extremes, or indeed to indulge in extreme sports in spectacular locations. If they did feel so inclined then there were always sensory replications of speed skating on the frozen moons of Platos or climbing the active volcanoes of Ignos, which were very high and regularly spewed forth lava smelling strongly of sulphur dioxide. Romana had tried these on occasion, and found them moderately enjoyable. But with nothing like that to look forward to here, she decided to concentrate on the job in hand. Get on with it and get out was the thing to do.

She flourished the Tracer and was rewarded with an electronic buzz. 'The target seems to be over there,' she told the Doctor. 'Let's go and find it.'

The Doctor set off immediately, leading the way across the moor at a brisk pace, with Romana floundering behind. To her considerable relief he suddenly paused and knelt down to examine the ground. Presently she found him prodding a series of deep indentations in the heather. They looked like the tracks of some huge beast, and they led in the direction of an ancient stone circle, which had just become visible on the brow of the hill.

'Wonder what made these,' murmured the Doctor.

'Elephants?' suggested Romana, who had done some rudimentary research on Earth fauna.

'There aren't any elephants in these parts.'

'Well, something very big and very heavy. Whatever it was, it must have weighed well over ten tons,' she replied. 'Perhaps the animals have put on weight since you were last here. If we hurry, perhaps we can grab the next segment of the Key before whatever it is comes back. I personally would prefer not to meet any animal that's this big.'

'The Earth has seen much bigger animals, you know,' observed the Doctor. 'But they all died out millions of years ago.'

'Maybe this one didn't. Do let's go and get this third segment, and then we can be off.'

Romana could see that if she didn't get the Doctor back on track, he would spend his time happily pottering on his favourite planet, finding trivial issues to delay his completion of their mission. People on Gallifrey had warned her about his inexhaustible curiosity. Then it came to her: distract him. It worked with children – why not with the Doctor? She pointed to the stones on the nearby hill.

'Look,' she said. 'They're interesting.' She waved the Tracer in the general direction of the stones and was rewarded with an answering buzz.

'Come on,' said the Doctor suddenly. 'Don't dilly-dally. Let's go and have a look.' And off he dashed.

When Romana, hampered by her choice of sling-backs, finally caught up with him, he was carefully examining the stones.

'Know what this is?' he demanded excitedly.

'A stone circle.'

He grunted. 'Know what it's for?'

'Playing games in?'

'Don't be ridiculous.' He almost embraced one of the pillars. 'This is a miracle of Bronze Age engineering. It's a megalithic temple-cum-observatory.'

Romana looked round scornfully. 'What are they supposed to be observing?' she asked.

'The sky, of course,' replied the Doctor testily.

'But they're just stones. How can they observe anything? Or am I missing something?'

'Several thousand years of Earth history, if you ask me,' he muttered. He looked round the circle with some pride. One of the reasons he liked Earth so much was that its inhabitants indulged in some very odd practices, like steam locomotion and synchronised swimming. You never knew what they would get up to next. Never a dull moment on Earth – if you didn't count the rain, of course.

'What you have here,' he explained, 'is a collection of monoliths aligned with various points on the horizon. If you know how to use them, they can predict sunrise and moonrise at different times of the year. Not to mention the solstices.'

Romana was still not impressed. 'I didn't realise the people here were so primitive.'

'Not *now*,' insisted the Doctor. 'These stones were erected thousands of years ago. Partly for religious reasons, of course. To keep in with the gods, not to mention the neighbours' gods as well. But also because they had no calendars. With these stones they could keep track of the seasons. It was a sort of sundial clock. With some of these circles they could even calculate eclipses.'

'Fascinating,' said Romana, with barely disguised sarcasm. 'Do you think one of these monoliths is the third segment?'

The Doctor shrugged. 'Who knows?'

Romana tried the Tracer once again, but with no response, which was odd because the thing had earlier reacted positively. Did that mean that the missing segment was part of a moving object, like a bird or a person? Even odder was the hooded figure in white which silently appeared from between two of the stones, like something out of a mystery thriller.

'Who are you?' Romana asked, momentarily taken aback.

The figure threw back the hood and revealed the features of a formidable lady in her sixties.

'I might well ask the same question,' the newcomer countered. She was apparently unhappy about finding anyone in the circle. 'This is National Trust property,' she declared, as if this would give her title to the site, but rather spoilt the effect by admitting, 'or will be when the politicians get around to it, although lord knows when that will be.'

Observing Romana hastily slipping the Tracer into her pocket, she demanded, 'What's that thing, girl? You do know this has all been surveyed.'

The Doctor, who had been examining various individual stones and largely ignoring Romana's involvement with the fierce-looking lady, decided to intervene.

'Surveyed?' he queried, taking in her snug white duffel coat and practical shoes.

The woman's lively, intelligent eyes glinted. 'Yes,

surveyed. This circle. Many times. By professionals. Or what passes for professionals these blighted days.'

The Doctor had no idea what she was talking about, but he nodded in a knowledgeable fashion which seemed to encourage her because she immediately became excited.

'Ah, you've noticed it too,' she exclaimed.

The Doctor chose to smile enigmatically, and looked hopefully in Romana's direction. But she shook her head and shrugged, equally clueless.

'I knew it was only a matter of time before another professional noticed the discrepancies,' the woman continued. She peered short-sightedly at him, recognition dawning. 'I know you, don't I?' she said taking his arm. 'We've met before somewhere ... Professor ... er-er-er ...'

'Doctor,' he murmured.

'Of course, of course. Doctor ... er-er-er ... Don't tell me. I've got a wonderful memory for faces. Never forget a face ... Doctor ... er-er ... I know – fogous. I associate you with fogous.'

'Fogous?'

'Fogous. That was it,' she declared. 'Cornish fogous. You read a paper on them at that symposium at Princeton. Or was it Cardiff? Or was it that fool Leamington-Smith who read it?' She studied him closely once again. 'You look nothing like him,' she concluded accusingly. 'He is small and fat and has a silly little beard. Anyway, the paper was dreadful. Complete tosh!'

'Sorry to hear it,' said the Doctor.

'Don't be. What would surprise me was if it was any good. The man's an idiot. Wears suede boots and green corduroys.'

Having dismissed Leamington-Smith to her own satisfaction, she paused for breath. In the interim, the Doctor took the opportunity to ask who she was.

'Professor Emilia Rumford,' she replied.

The Doctor looked blank.

'Rumford,' she repeated hopefully. 'R-U-M-F-O-R-D. As in the author of *Bronze Age Burials in Gloucestershire*.'

'Ah, the definitive work on the subject!' declared the Doctor with sudden vigour. He had never heard of the book, but it was better than pleading ignorance. The Doctor's previous experience of academics had convinced him that a little flattery got you everywhere. It certainly seemed to put him into Professor Rumford's good books. She positively beamed.

'You're too kind, Doctor,' she replied modestly. 'Not that I'm going to pretend that you're not absolutely correct, of course. But praise from a fellow professional is always gratifying. It was Dr Borlase's survey of 1754 that alerted you to it, wasn't it?'

The Doctor was finding the Professor's thought processes hard to follow. Who was Dr Borlase and what did he have to do with anything? Again, the Doctor tried hard to look modest rather than bewildered, and apparently succeeded because the Professor ploughed on regardless. 'That's how I twigged it. When I came to compare Dr Borlase with the Rev. Thomas Bright's survey of 1820,' she said. 'And then the two surveys of 1876 and 1911 – well, it was obvious, wasn't it?'

The Doctor and Romana looked at each other in total bewilderment and said with one voice: 'What was obvious?'

There followed an expectant silence. Realising that the Professor was waiting for a formal introduction, the Doctor did the honours. 'My assistant, Romana.'

The Professor's lined face crinkled in a welcoming smile. 'Hello. Charming name. What's its origin, I wonder?'

But Romana could see where all this was leading. If she wasn't careful, they would soon be knee-deep in the history of nomenclature. And they hadn't time for it. 'What was obvious?' she repeated.

The Professor looked surprised. 'Why, that on more than one occasion there had been a miscount, my dear,' she said.

'Of what?' demanded Romana.

'Of the stones, of course. According to Dr Borlase the Nine Travellers here –' she indicated the stones – 'that's what the locals call them . . . well, according to Borlase, they were only six in number . . .'

'But there are definitely nine stones here,' asserted Romana, realising at last what the Professor was getting at.

'Good girl!' exclaimed Professor Rumford, as if rewarding a backward person for working out that two plus two did after all equal four. 'You've got it. The Travellers got their name because there were nine of them – still are today – yet several historians record there only being six. Curious, isn't it?'

The Doctor was on his knees examining a patch of unusually stained grass by the central altar stone. 'So's this,' he said.

'What?' asked the Professor, bending down to study the stain too.

'Dried blood,' explained the Doctor. 'Quite a lot of it. It looks as if some animal had its throat cut here. On the altar stone.'

Unheard by all of them, a dark-haired, striking-looking woman in her thirties had entered the circle. Professor Rumford looked up and smiled.

'Ah, Vivien,' she said to the newcomer. 'Glad you could make it.' Then, turning to the Doctor, she went on, 'Doctor, this is my friend, Miss Fay,' she concluded. 'Another Somerville girl, as you might expect.'

The Doctor doffed his hat and bowed. 'Congratulations. You move very quietly, Miss Fay. I didn't hear you approach.'

'I used to be a Brown Owl,' she replied.

Recalling her study of Earth fauna, Romana was puzzled. 'A brown owl?'

'Leader of a Brownie pack,' explained the Doctor, sotto voce. Then, seeing his assistant's incomprehension, he added, 'Explanations later.' He turned back to Miss Fay. 'We found this stain in the grass. I'm afraid it's a little grisly.'

Miss Fay was not discomposed by the sight of blood. 'Oh, it'll probably be just another sacrifice,' she replied. 'Nothing to worry about.'

'Nothing to worry about!' gasped Romana. 'Doctor, you told me Earth was quite civilised now.'

The Doctor shushed her and turned to Miss Fay. 'Do you mean to say there have been other sacrifices at these stones?'

Professor Rumford's friend gave him an utterly charming smile. 'It's just the BIDS having fun,' she said. 'Quite harmless.'

'Who are the Bids?' asked Romana.

'The British Institute of Druidic studies,' explained Miss Fay. 'Nothing to do with real druids, of course, past or present. They're just a group of oddballs who meet here regularly. They wear white robes and wave bits of mistletoe and curved knives around and slaughter the odd chicken on the altar. As the Professor will tell you, it's all very unhistorical.'

But Professor Rumford wasn't so sure. 'I don't think you can dismiss them quite so easily, Vivien,' she said.

'Recently, they're supposed to have got more ambitious and killed the odd sheep.'

'That can't please the local farmers,' observed the Doctor.

'Oh, they buy them first, of course,' said Miss Fay. 'They don't go in for sheep stealing. It's all above board.'

The Doctor regarded Miss Fay quizzically. 'You seem very well informed.'

'It was all written up recently in a Sunday newspaper,' the woman replied, sharing a mischievous look with her friend. 'Emilia and I read it with inappropriate glee.'

The idea of these two poring over the weekly scandal sheets amused the Doctor. Grinning roguishly at the older academic, he enquired, 'Have you had any trouble with them, Professor?'

Professor Rumford frowned, recalling several incidents with the BIDS in the past. 'A bit,' she admitted. 'Their leader, a Mr de Vries, is a very unpleasant man. He's always objecting to people coming here. Says it upsets the "etherous" vibrations of the place. Whatever that might mean.'

Miss Fay smiled indulgently at her friend, and went on, 'Emilia has little time for sloppy thinking, Doctor. In her view a measuring tape and a theodolite are all you need to establish the facts of any archaeological site. Measure. Record. And come to your conclusions in the cold light of reason – that's what you tell your students, isn't it, Emilia?'

The Professor sniffed. 'Not that I have many these days. Fewer and fewer young people seemed prepared to devote time and energy to serious analysis of the Bronze Age.'

Miss Fay continued, 'Mr de Vries says that this place should be regarded as a temple, and treated with all due reverence as if it were still a holy place. Which I suppose, to the BIDS, it is.'

'They chant, you know,' interjected Professor Rumford. 'Ridiculous habit. There's no way they can know what rites were celebrated here. Let alone what language was used. All the BIDS do is dress up in white bedsheets and dance around the stones, shouting a lot of nonsense. All mumbo-jumbo.' She chuckled. 'Must cost a fortune in laundry bills, though.'

'As a matter of fact,' said Miss Fay, 'we thought that you might be more members of Mr de Vries's group.'

'No bedsheets,' pointed out the Doctor. 'No chanting.'

'Jolly good thing, too,' observed Professor Rumford. 'You see, Vivien and I are conducting a complete topographical, geological, astronomical and archaeological survey of the site.'

Before she could go on, the Doctor asked, 'How can I meet this Mr de Vries? Where does he live?'

'Nearby,' replied the Professor. 'He lives at the big house just over the hill. Bodcombe Manor, it is called. He bought it or inherited it – I can't remember which – a few years ago. Great barn of a place. Must cost the BIDS a fortune to heat it. Still, that's their problem.'

'How do I get there?'

'Just follow that path.' She indicated a well-trodden track that led up the hill. 'It'll take you about twenty minutes. It can be quite hard going, you know. Still you're a big strapping fellow, so you should be all right.'

'You're not going to see Mr de Vries now, are you?' Romana asked plaintively. She didn't fancy another long walk up a hill, and certainly not in her heels. She briefly contemplated going barefoot. It wasn't an attractive prospect.

But the Doctor had made his mind up. 'Strike while the iron is hot. Don't put off today what you can put off tomorrow. Or have I got that quite right?'

Professor Rumford ventured, 'I think I should warn you, Doctor, that Mr de Vries doesn't like visitors. Particularly scientists.'

'Well, he's not alone in that. Very few people do in my experience!' Then, changing the subject in a way that Romana always found infuriating, he suddenly asked, 'Have you noticed those indentations in the ground back there, Professor? What do you make of them?'

Professor Rumford was dismissive. 'Probably one of the local farmers moving equipment.'

'Yes,' replied the Doctor. 'I'm sure you're right. But a

bit odd, nevertheless.' He indicated the track. 'This way, you say?'

Professor Rumford nodded. 'Couple of miles at the most.'

'Two miles!' exclaimed Romana, aghast. 'In these shoes?'

'Well, I did warn you. They're not the thing for hiking.'

Miss Fay agreed with the Doctor. 'Not very practical, are they?'

The Doctor, eyebrow raised, shook his head in a manner guaranteed to infuriate a saint. 'She wouldn't be told, you know.'

Romana simply glared at him.

Professor Rumford came up with a diplomatic solution. She said to Romana, 'Why don't you hang on here? That would be all right, wouldn't it?'

'I'll stop off on the way back and fetch some boots.' Drawing Romana to one side, the Doctor lowered his voice to a whisper. 'If I were you I'd keep an eye on these two. There's something very odd going on.'

Romana nodded. There was nothing of tangible concern about the Professor and Miss Fay, but they just seemed a little bit . . . odd. She was pleased the Doctor felt the same way.

'What shall I do if anything does happen?' she replied softly.

'Scream. Yell. Run like the wind.'

She had a feeling he was teasing her, but she simply nodded.

'Right,' said the Doctor loudly, preparing to take his leave. 'Just over the hill, you said, Professor? I shouldn't be long, Romana. Adieu.'

With that he flung his long scarf round his neck and strode out of the circle and up the path to Bodcombe Manor.

'Typical,' snorted Miss Fay. 'Typical male behaviour. Strands you here in the middle of nowhere with two complete strangers while he goes off to enjoy himself with Mr de Vries.'

'From what I know of De Vries,' said the Professor, gravely, 'the Doctor is welcome to him. Seeing him is not my idea of a jolly time. Anyway,' she went on, 'we've got more important things to do.' She turned to Romana. 'Perhaps, my dear, you'd like to help us to work while you're waiting. It's just taking measurements.'

'Oh, I can do that,' replied Romana, glad to be of use. Measuring, she understood.

'Jolly good. Let's get cracking then.'

On the way to the manor, the Doctor paused to examine the strange indentations again. There was no way they were made by farm machinery, he decided. Another mystery. Perhaps De Vries might know the answer.

Suddenly he noticed several large, black birds, flying

low over his head, crowing angrily. He waved the end of his long scarf at them.

'Go away!' he shouted. 'Shoo!' But the birds paid no attention and continued to pester him all the way to Bodcombe Manor.

Back at the circle, Romana was helping Professor Rumford and Miss Fay to measure each monolith – by height, width and position relative to the other stones. The aim was to establish the exact proportions of the site. The Professor dashed about fussily, all the while flourishing a large extending measuring tape, the size and shape of an Olympic discus. Periodically she paused to bark instructions to Romana or Miss Fay, or to confirm measurements which Miss Fay recorded in a notebook.

'All this was here for a reason,' she told Romana, gesturing to the stones that surrounded them. 'Our job is to establish the facts – precisely what is here now. How it aligns with the landscape and so forth. Only once we've done that can we begin to theorise about what it's here for: what the people who built it intended it to do. You've got to remember that a stone circle took a long time to build. It was a major engineering project for any Bronze Age tribe to undertake. A stone circle is a kind of machine. It's a calendar, a rosary, a star chart and a church all in one.'

She paused for a moment to watch Miss Fay take

the other end of her tape measure and place it against one of the stones.

'Are you sure that's straight, Vivien?'

Miss Fay gave her a thumbs-up sign.

'Jolly good. What's the measurement? Twenty-eight-point-nine metres.' Miss Fay took her notebook and entered the numbers therein.

Romana straightened her aching back and was startled to hear a sudden cawing and a flurry of wings. Looking up, she saw a large black bird perch on the stone that towered over her. 'What's that?' she said uneasily.

'Only a crow,' replied Miss Fay. 'There are lots of them around here. Nothing to be afraid of.'

But Romana wasn't so sure. The crow was looking down on her almost as if she was potential prey. She waved her hand lamely, but it ignored her. Soon the crow was joined on top of the stone by another two. All three now glared at her malevolently.

Against her better judgement, Romana shivered.

Chapter III

The British Institute of Druidic Studies

In a darkened room across the moor, a brazier suddenly burst into flame. It illuminated a small altar on which lay a goblet, a large bunch of mistletoe and a sickle whose blade had been honed to razor sharpness: all the tools required by a Druid priest to perform a sacrifice in honour of his gods. To complete the scene, two hooded, white-robed figures emerged from the shadows: the priest and his acolyte. Now they waited for a sign that their deity was present and the ceremony could begin.

The figures pushed back their hoods, revealing themselves to be Mr de Vries, a plump man sporting a wisp of a beard on his chin, and Martha Vickers, a middle-aged lady with the face of a discontented bull-dog. She was a resident of the nearby village of Bodcombe Parva, and a member of the local Women's Institute. Her fellow members would have been astonished to see her there, because she was known to be non-religious and only sang 'Jerusalem' under protest. In fact, ever since meeting Mr de Vries a couple of years ago, she had been a pillar of his Druid circle, gradually initiated into the inner mysteries of the BIDS. She used to hunt in her younger days, and unlike some of the other group members was not disturbed by the sight of blood. Hence her presence at all the sacrifices.

Presently Mr de Vries began to chant. 'Cailleach! Cailleach! Cailleach! Great Goddess! We come to do your bidding.'

He nodded to Martha, who joined in gamely with, 'O Cailleach. O Cailleach. Come amongst us so that we may do your bidding.'

As if in reply, there came the sound of a loud fluttering of wings and the harsh cawing of a large bird, and a raven suddenly appeared out of the darkness and came to rest on a wooden stand beside the altar.

The deity was now present. The two worshippers bowed to the raven. The ceremony could begin.

The Doctor paused at the iron-gated entrance to the manor and admired the building from afar. It was a large, half-timbered manor house clearly dating from the late seventeenth century. Though there had been later additions to the property, it still retained its original features. By any standards, it was a beautiful house. The only things the Doctor found off-putting were the presence of a raven, which eyed him beadily while perched on top of the gate, and the wording of a brass plaque attached to the gates. It read:

BRITISH INSTITUTE OF DRUIDIC STUDIES
ANTON DE VRIES, PRINCIPAL
NO VISITORS UNLESS BY PREVIOUS APPOINTMENT

The bird flew away, cawing indignantly, when the Doctor pushed open the gates. He studied the plaque again. A bit unfriendly, he thought. It couldn't be easy to gain adherents to your cause if you didn't welcome visitors. What was De Vries afraid of?

He set off up the long gravel drive to the manor. The way was narrow and lined on both sides with laurel and rhododendrons, which made for a gloomy approach to the house. It looked more like a set from a horror film than the headquarters of a quasi-religious institute. The Doctor rang the big brass bell beside the door. He waited but heard nothing. He rang again: still no answer.

This is no way to run an academy, he thought. Where are the students? And the professors? The place should have been humming with activity.

He tried the front door, and it swung open onto a long, dark hallway.

'Hello,' he called. 'Anyone at home? Yoo-hoo!'

He peered in. No Count Dracula, no Frankenstein's Monster. Just a lot of rather grimy paintings hanging on the walls, and some equally dusty Jacobean tables and straight-backed chairs.

'Obviously you can't get reliable staff around here,'

the Doctor said to himself. Whatever abstract cerebration might be going on elsewhere, the Institute was not a house of physical activity. He coughed. He whistled. He called out. But no one appeared. In the end, he decided to go and look at the paintings. These turned out to be portraits of previous owners of the manor, many of whom, the Doctor noticed, were women.

In a painting labelled *The original Lord Montcalm*, the house's founder stood surrounded by his family, his wife and two rather plain daughters. He looked like a man who enjoyed the good things of life. Oddly, there was a patch of lighter wallpaper where the next portrait should have hung – and two more further along.

The Doctor was attracted to a portrait of an eighteenth-century divine. He was a smiling fellow, in a parson's robes. A serious man, but clearly no fool. The Doctor found his appearance sympathetic. The plaque beneath the painting declared him to be *Doctor Thomas Borlase, 1701–1754*.

'So that's the good doctor,' he said aloud.

'Indeed,' replied a voice behind him.

The Doctor turned to find himself face to face with a smallish, plump man with a wisp of a beard. He was recognisable from Professor Rumford's description.

'Mr de Vries, I presume.'

'Correct, Doctor,' replied the other.

'I do hope you'll forgive my intrusion. I did knock, but nobody came.'

Mr de Vries nodded and said mildly, 'So you decided to help yourself. I see you're studying the portraits of the inestimable Dr Borlase.'

The Doctor graciously inclined his head. 'A fine-looking chap. He surveyed the Nine Travellers, I believe, but got his sums wrong. Still, Professor Rumford seems to think highly of him.'

De Vries smiled rather condescendingly. 'Yes, I'm sure she does,' he replied. 'He's the sort of person she would approve of. He measured things, you know. Emilia likes people who measure things. She thinks that's important.'

'Oh, but it is,' declared the Doctor. 'Without people who measure things, think of all the ill-fitting suits we'd have to wear.'

But Mr de Vries was not amused. 'It was very sad about Dr Borlase,' he said. 'Did Emilia tell you?'

'No. What happened to him?'

'One of the biggest stones fell on him while he was completing his survey. Crushed him to death. Rather an appropriate end, I always think. Another measurer bites the dust.'

'Maybe we should warn the Professor?'

'Oh, no, no, no, I'm sure she'll be quite safe so long as she doesn't do anything to disturb the stones.'

'In what way?'

'Poking around,' explained De Vries. 'Generally disturbing them. You know.'

Noting what appeared to be an unvoiced threat in De Vries's reply, the Doctor changed the subject. He pointed to the blank spaces on the wall. 'I'm intrigued by the missing pictures. Where are they?'

'Being cleaned,' replied De Vries. 'They were in quite a bad state, I'm afraid. The one of Lady Montcalm – the so-called wicked Lady Montcalm who is supposed to have murdered several husbands on their wedding nights – that one we were told was quite valuable. Experts think it may be by a pupil of Van Dyck.'

'What were the other pictures, then?' asked the Doctor, ever curious. 'Portraits of the unfortunate husbands?'

'No, nothing so ghoulish. Just studies of two women – a Mrs Trefusis and a Senhora Camara. The first was a recluse who lived here for nearly fifty years with only birds for company. Senhora Camara was the widow of a Brazilian millionaire. She was very rich and very generous, and as a result much loved by the locals.'

'Do we know what happened to Senhor Camara?'

'He fell overboard on his voyage from Brazil.'

'Obviously a risky business, being married to one of these ladies,' observed the Doctor.

'Nothing is known about any husband of Mrs Trefusis.'

'So she must have got rid of him early.'

De Vries smiled gently, now at last apparently warming to the Doctor. 'Why are we standing around in the hall? Let me offer a glass of sherry.'

'How very hospitable of you,' replied the Doctor, looking forward to seeing more of the house. 'Yes, I should like that very much . . .'

By late afternoon Romana was feeling exhausted. She seemed to have been measuring the stones, driving in marking stakes and taking further measurements with Professor Rumford's theodolite for hours. Her back ached, her head hurt and she needed a hot bath.

'These crows have been circling around us all afternoon,' she remarked to Professor Rumford, who nodded absently.

'Yes,' agreed the Professor. 'But this was a sacred place once. Perhaps the birds still have a memory of it as a food source.'

'You mean they would feed on what was left after the sacrifices?'

'Of course,' said the Professor. 'If you're a sacrifice in human eyes, then you're just so much meat to a hungry crow. Anyway, thanks for all your help, Romana. Fancy a mug of tea and some sandwiches?'

Romana considered. She had no experience of Earth food, yet somehow the prospect seemed delightful. But where was the Doctor? Surely he ought to be back by now?

'Do come,' said Miss Fay, her smile as charming as ever. 'My cottage is just over the hill. Tea and hot buttered crumpets await.'

Romana had never wanted a hot buttered crumpet more, whatever it might be. The cuisine on Gallifrey – especially for trainee Time Lords – tended to be rather bland and basic, and no doubt the Doctor would wax lyrical about Terran sustenance. Temptation beckoned, but she resisted.

'No,' she said. 'Thank you very much. But I'd better wait here for the Doctor to return. Otherwise he won't know where I am.'

'Please yourself, girl,' remarked the Professor. 'But if you change your mind, we're not far away.' With that she took hold of one end of a wicker laundry basket into which they had packed the various odds and ends needed for the survey of the stones.

Miss Fay hastily took the other end of the basket, but paused smiling at Romana. 'Do bring your friend with you, when he gets back,' she said.

'Yes, of course. Thank you.'

'Lift, Vivien, lift,' directed Professor Rumford. Together the two women staggered off, carrying the basket between them.

Left on her own at last, Romana walked slowly round the circle, touching each of the stones with the wand-like Tracer, without result. Nothing to indicate that the missing segment of the Key to Time was present anywhere. Her activities seemed to attract the interest of the birds, however. More and more came to circle overhead. Once again, she shivered in spite of herself, unable to stop herself feeling that they somehow presaged trouble.

Meanwhile, the Doctor was enjoying a glass of sherry with Mr de Vries while following him on a conducted tour of the old house, which in fact was proving rather boring. He'd seen nothing more sinister than a couple of classrooms and a dormitory for visiting students, of which there were none in evidence.

'The Druid business a bit slow at the moment, is it?' he enquired, all sympathy.

'It has its ups and downs, of course,' agreed De Vries. 'Next week we should be full up. There's a group coming from Liverpool.'

The Doctor stopped in his tracks. 'Not The Beatles?' He grinned broadly. 'Wouldn't The Rolling Stones be more appropriate?'

Apparently deciding to ignore such poor humour, De Vries led him down the corridor to where some heavy curtains barred the way. 'Welcome to our holy of holies,' he said rather grandly and parted the curtains.

Beyond lay a large room, filled with late-afternoon sunlight. At one end of the room stood an altar, on it a large copper bowl and a curved knife. Beside the altar, on a wooden perch, stood the largest raven the Doctor had ever seen.

'That's rather an unusual pet, isn't it?' he observed.

'It's not exactly what you'd call a pet, Doctor,' replied the other. 'More like a familiar.'

'I thought only witches had familiars. Or do Druids indulge in that kind of thing, too?'

'Druids are involved in many different activities.'

'I can imagine.' The Doctor returned to a subject he had wanted to raise ever since he met De Vries. 'I've been meaning to ask – how did you know my name? Did a little bird tell you? Or even a big one?'

De Vries's smile was without humour. 'And there's something I've been meaning to ask you, Doctor. What is your interest in the Nine Travellers? Not just curiosity, surely.'

'No,' agreed the Doctor. 'I'm looking for something. Part of a key.'

'A key to what?'

'Excellent question,' replied the Doctor. 'I wish I could help you. All I know is that it's part of a key that's just been mislaid. By the way,' he went on, having decided that he'd answered enough of De Vries' questions, 'you're not really a Druid, are you? Not in this day and age.'

'Not in the conventional sense, no,' agreed De Vries. 'I consider myself a humble student of Druidic lore.'

'There's not much of that surely,' the Doctor pointed out. 'We know so little about the Druids. Nothing that's historically reliable anyway. There's the odd mention in Julius Caesar and Tacitus. But no detail. Nothing you can get your teeth into. In fact, I always thought Druidism was invented by old John Aubrey in the seventeenth century, more as a joke than a serious attempt to add to the sum of human knowledge.'

For a moment, the Doctor was captivated by his own memories. He remembered the disreputable old diarist fondly. He had visited him many times, while the old man put away quantities of good red wine and regaled his visitor with the latest scandals about his contemporaries. 'Old John was the best scandalmonger since Suetonius gave us the lowdown on the Caesars,' he went on.

But De Vries was clearly offended by the Doctor's dismissal of his faith. 'Druidism is no joke,' he said stiffly.

'That's a pity,' replied the Doctor. 'So what's your interest in the stones?'

De Vries glared at him. 'The stones are sacred,' he declared. 'Holy things in a holy place.'

'To whom or to what are they sacred?'

'To one who is mighty and all-powerful. To the Goddess!'

The Doctor looked sceptical. 'Oh yes? What goddess would that be?'

'She has many names,' explained De Vries. A fanatical look had appeared in his eyes. 'Morriga ... Hermentana ... But those who serve her today call her the Cailleach.'

The Doctor identified the deity immediately. 'Celtic. Of course. One of those Irish goddesses the Church took over. Probably a Saint now. St Cailleach of Kerry . . .' He thought about it for a moment. 'Sounds possible.'

But not to De Vries. 'The Cailleach,' he declared, 'is the Goddess of War. Death. And Magic . . .' Seeing the Doctor about to stroke the raven's head, he said urgently, 'Don't, Doctor. Beware the crow and the raven; they are the eyes of the Cailleach.' Warily, he eyed the glistening beak, which even now was aiming towards soft flesh.

The Doctor withdrew his hand immediately, causing the large bird to miss its target. It flapped its wings irritably, trying to remain on its perch.

'You don't really believe all that rubbish, do you?' said the Doctor. 'I mean, I'm all in favour of the old gods and goddesses, but surely in this day and age the Cailleach is well and truly past her sell-by date.'

'You still don't understand, do you, Doctor?'

De Vries took the Doctor's arm and led him towards the curtained end of the room. 'I have seen her power. And now so shall you.' He swept aside the curtains.

Standing behind the altar, arms outstretched, was a strange, terrifying figure, robed in white, with a black feathered bird mask covering its face, like some half-human bird. As the Doctor turned back to De Vries, he realised too late that the latter had grasped the copper bowl in both hands and was now bringing it down on his head with a resounding thump.

Before the Doctor passed out, he glimpsed the bird-masked Goddess kneel beside him. She touched him with a black gloved hand. Attached to the gloves were talons which scratched his cheek.

Romana was still in the circle, awaiting the arrival of the Doctor. He was worryingly late. She heard something approaching and looked in the direction of the noise. Suddenly she seemed to be surrounded by mist which obscured her vision. A figure formed out of the mist. A familiar figure.

'Doctor,' she said, 'where have you been?'

But there was no reply.

'Doctor? Are you all right?'

Again, no reaction. It seemed to her that he was beckoning for her to follow him away from the circle and into the mist. She started to follow, but found her high-heeled shoes impeded her progress, so she kicked them off and ran after him in bare feet, ignoring the small stones and tough, tussocky gorse. She had almost caught up with him when she heard the sound of the sea. They must be near a clifftop, she thought. Where was he leading her? Were they being pursued?

She looked around, but there seemed to be no one behind them. Suddenly the cliff edge reared up in front of her, the ground falling away just metres from where she stood. But of the Doctor there was no sign. Romana stood as close to the cliff edge as she dared, and looked down, hoping desperately that the Doctor hadn't fallen. But she had heard no cry, seen nothing. The sea churned noisily away hundreds of metres below, and the wind whipped in from across the water.

She cried out, 'Doctor! Where are you? Are you all right? Are you hurt?'

He had been in front of her, and she'd followed him to this spot. It didn't make sense for him to have simply vanished. Steeling her nerves, she knelt and peered more closely over the cliff edge, frightened that he might be lying amongst the rocks down below. Perhaps he was badly hurt; dead, even. As a child she had nursed the absurd illusion that Time Lords were immortal. They weren't, of course.

Just for a moment, she thought she heard laughter behind her. Standing, she half turned towards the sound and saw a tall figure looming out of the mist. It went for her with frightening speed, its full weight careering into her.

'Doctor! No!' she screamed, as she fought against the figure. But it was no good – her bare feet skidded on the grass, and she quickly slipped over the edge of the cliff, desperately scrabbling for something to hang on to. The edge of the ground winded her as she hit it, and as she slid away from it she grabbed hold of a slender bush growing from the lip of the cliff face. It impeded her fall slightly, but soon came away in her hand. As her feet tried to claw at the bare rock, she grabbed on to a series of scrubby bushes until, as if rewarded by a miracle, she suddenly came to rest on a small ledge about three metres down. The waves thundered below, and the gusting wind tore at her back. It was all she could do to cling on to the outcrops of rock and plant life. There was no chance of moving, and certainly not of climbing back up unaided. Unless somebody rescued her, she was finished.

Suddenly something buffeted her back. She looked round and saw that it was a gull. The creature seemed to be trying to push her off the ledge. Soon more gulls appeared screeching and buffeting her with their wings. Romana closed her eyes and screamed again for help.

Darkness was beginning to fall as the Doctor, still unconscious from the blow to his head, and now bound hand and foot as well, was wheeled across the moor on a small pushcart that the gardener at the manor normally used to move plant pots. A couple of white-robed acolytes were doing the pushing and finding it hard going because of the uneven ground.

Meanwhile De Vries led the procession, with the faithful Martha by his side. Other acolytes brought up the rear, chanting in the manner that Professor Rumford found so offensive. Once inside the circle of stones, the procession halted and, at a signal from De Vries, transferred the recumbent figure from cart to great altar stone.

With the scene now clearly set for the sacrifice, De Vries produced an ornate bronze bowl and placed it by the Doctor's head, alongside a large, curved knife wrapped in scarlet silk. Martha, who occasionally wore the robes of the Goddess when required, as she had done earlier in the altar room, was one of De Vries's most trusted followers, but at the moment she wasn't happy. She was scared that things were getting out of hand.

'Look,' she said. 'You can't do this, Anton. It's murder.'

De Vries, already under the spell of Cailleach, answered as if in a dream. 'It is the will of the Goddess.'

Martha persevered. 'If it is, we'll all end up in prison. You, me and everyone here. Surely you don't want that. *She* doesn't want that.'

'Who are we to oppose the Goddess's will?' intoned De Vries. 'The Cailleach demands blood.'

Martha's voice betrayed the fear she now felt. 'She's never demanded human sacrifice before.'

'Well now she has,' declared De Vries. 'I daren't oppose her will, Martha. I daren't.' He couldn't look at her. 'The Cailleach neither forgives nor forgets failure to follow her orders. And I have sworn to obey her. We all have.'

Martha was on the verge of panic. She had joined

De Vries's group because it promised to be more exciting than the WI: at least she wasn't expected to sing that awful 'Jerusalem'. She didn't mind the occasional blood sacrifice, so long as they were animals. After all, her father had shot practically every species on the face of the planet. But even he drew the line at people, which had not made him popular with the authorities in two wars. No one could understand how a man who had shot everything from quail to quagga could draw the line at people. 'But people,' Daddy had said to her, 'are different: *we* are people. And I wouldn't ever shoot you, darling.'

No, thought Martha, at least you were safe with Daddy.

'It is the Cailleach's will,' insisted De Vries again.

'How do we know?' demanded Martha. 'She isn't here to tell us. She isn't here to explain.'

Though in truth, she realised, the Cailleach never explained. She commanded. She gave orders her followers were expected to obey. At first Martha had found this rather refreshing: there was a distinct lack of discipline in the country today. But she was no fool and had just begun to see how this Cailleach worship could be dangerous.

'She will come,' bleated De Vries. 'The Cailleach will come.'

'But so will *his* people.' Martha pointed at the Doctor. 'He will have friends. They will miss him. They will go to the police, they'll trace him here and we'll all be arrested.'

De Vries was in no mood to listen to the voice of reason. 'The Cailleach will have foreseen everything. The Doctor will not be missed. Have faith in the Cailleach. You will see. She will come.'

De Vries lifted the curved knife. He prepared to cut the Doctor's throat from ear to ear.

Chapter IV

Inside the Circle

Before the blade could be brought down, the Doctor spoilt the whole effect by regaining consciousness and saying, 'Hello, you're Mr de Vries, aren't you? The one who bashed me on the head. Not very druidic of you, was it?' He inspected the knife hovering a few inches from his throat. 'I do hope that thing's been properly sterilised.'

'Blasphemer,' screamed De Vries, still trying to work up the courage to plunge the knife into the Doctor's throat.

'No. Just careful,' replied the Doctor. 'You can get all sorts of nasty infections from a dirty sacrificial knife. To begin with, there's tetanus, not to mention a whole host of unpleasant staphylococci.'

Realising that De Vries's grand scheme had by now gone pear-shaped, Martha decided to seek the nearest exit. Suddenly the prospect of singing hymns in polite company seemed quite attractive. Of course, she would miss the mistletoe and the mead and the occasional orgy with the BIDS, but at least in the WI you didn't normally land up in prison. Besides, she said to herself, remember you're the daughter of a big game hunter. Once upon a time the name Vickers Shikari had meant something in the foothills of the Himalayas. Not to mention Kenya and Rhodesia and, indeed, wherever a hunter raised a gun to bring down his prey. So what on earth are you doing with this scruffy, unwashed lot?

Because you hoped one day Anton would put you ahead of his beliefs, she realised, with sad and sudden clarity.

'Don't be a fool,' she said to De Vries. 'It's not too late. Let him go.'

'I wouldn't hang about if I was you,' called the Doctor, raising his voice so all the acolytes could hear. 'Any of you. Suppose the police turn up. I can see the headlines now – SECRET DRUIDIC RAVE. GHOULISH RITES ON SACRED PROPERTY. DOZENS ARRESTED.'

'Shut up,' shouted De Vries. But as he looked round he could see the acolytes already divesting themselves of their robes and beginning to sidle away. Even the faithful Martha was making excuses and turning away. Soon there was only him standing over the Doctor, knife in hand, and feeling dangerously exposed.

'Before you decide to do anything particularly silly,' interjected the Doctor, 'I have a question. Does your Cailleach ride a bicycle?'

'Bicycle?' echoed De Vries, now totally bewildered. 'Of course she doesn't. Is there no end to your blasphemies?'

'If she doesn't,' went on the Doctor, 'then who's that I see approaching on a bike? An inspector from the Office of Unlicensed Sacrifices?'

De Vries looked round hastily, and sure enough, a figure on a bicycle could be seen approaching the circle at a fast wobble. He made an instant decision, grabbed up the instruments of sacrifice and set off in the direction of the manor at a gallop, his white-robed figure rapidly fading from view in the darkness.

'Don't forget your pushcart!' yelled the Doctor, ever helpful. 'Oh well,' he added when he was ignored. 'I suppose you can always come back for it later.' He rolled about on top of the altar trying to see the identity of his cycling saviour, but found he couldn't move far because of the ropes. He called out: 'Help! Help! Over here!'

He was delighted to see Professor Rumford dismounting from an old boneshaker of a bike equipped with wicker baskets fore and aft. At the same time he could hear car engines starting up nearby, as several members of the British Institute of Druidic Studies tried to urgently return to their homes.

'Good grief, man,' demanded the Professor, 'what are you doing? You'll catch your death of cold lying there.'

'You know how it is, Professor – one gets so tied up

in one's work.' The Doctor watched for a moment as she fumbled unsuccessfully with his bonds. 'Do you have a knife?' he enquired gently. 'It might be quicker.'

'Of course. What was I thinking of?' Producing a large clasp knife that Jack the Ripper might have envied from the folds of her duffel coat, the Professor began sawing away at the ropes. 'Who were those people?' she asked. 'It almost looked as if they were trying to cut your throat.'

'I think that was definitely one of their options,' he replied. 'But fortunately, Professor, you rode to the rescue. Incidentally, why did you come back?'

'To give Romana a break. She'd decided to wait here until you returned. I know how irresponsible you men can be, so I brought a flask of soup for her.'

The Doctor's tone of voice hardened. 'Then where is she now?'

Romana perched on the narrow ledge on the cliff face, overlooking a thirty-metre drop to the rocks and the sea. She was hanging on by her fingers and toes, calling for help. Fortunately, the gulls, having failed to push her off the ledge, seemed to have lost interest altogether. She was completely alone.

Standing in the stone circle with the Professor beside him, the Doctor was yelling at the top of his lungs.

'Romana! Romana . . . Halloo!'

They paused in silence for a moment, listening for an answering cry. But there was none.

'Maybe she was frightened by those wretched Druids and ran off,' suggested the Professor.

'I can't see a bunch of oddballs wrapped in bedsheets scaring Romana. She's as tough as the old boots she ought to be wearing.'

'Glad to hear it,' remarked the Professor. 'On the other hand, I won't want to be alarmist, Doctor, but there are several old mine workings on the moor. It can be quite dangerous, particularly at night. Oh, I do hope she hasn't gone wandering over the clifftops, the ground can be very treacherous there . . .'

The Doctor, spying Romana's discarded shoes half-hidden in a patch of tussock grass, stooped and picked them up. 'At least she ditched these.'

'Surely she can't have gone far without her shoes,' exclaimed the Professor. 'She should be somewhere nearby.'

'Romana?' called the Doctor again. 'Romana?'

But it was no use. The silence of the moor seemed infinite.

Professor Rumford called upon her practical background as one of the early girl guides. 'The only thing we can do is to organise a search party in the morning. I know a couple of local farmers who've got dogs that can follow a trail.'

The Doctor threw his arms around the Professor. 'A

dog! Of course! Professor – or may I call you Emilia? – you're a genius!'

'You have a dog?' enquired the Professor in some surprise. Somehow this strange academic hadn't struck her as a typical dog-lover. Surely, he was more a Pavlov than a Kennel Club devotee; an experimenter not a breeder. Still, these days you could never be sure.

'Have I got a dog!' exclaimed the Doctor. 'Just you wait and see.' He produced a small silver whistle from the pocket of his coat and blew a long, but inaudible, blast.

Emilia clapped her hands together. 'Oh! Is that one of those new-fangled whistles? They operate at a higher frequency than the human ear. Dogs can hear it but we can't. That's right, isn't it?'

'Something like that,' agreed the Doctor and blew soundlessly once again.

Inside the TARDIS, K-9 – who had put himself disconsolately into standby mode – reacted immediately to the Doctor's summons: all his circuits suddenly activated; his antennae quivered; lights flashed on and off. He was ready for action. At the little robot's command, the doors of the TARDIS opened and he trundled into the cool night air. Once outside, he paused to establish a set of precise coordinates, and then set off across the rough terrain.

*

'Tell you what, Professor,' said the Doctor. 'I'll leave you here and go off and meet my dog.'

'Will you be able to find him in the dark?'

'Oh yes, he's fully programmed. He could find me in the middle of a snowstorm if he had to.'

'Then he's a lot cleverer than most dogs I know. You'll have to give him a jolly big bone as a reward.'

'Something like that,' the Doctor agreed. 'If you could wait here, Professor, in case Romana should return shortly?'

'Don't worry, I'll hang on for the poor girl. You know,' she added, with a sudden little dance on the spot, 'it's all getting rather exciting, isn't it?'

'Let's hope it doesn't get too exciting,' said the Doctor, and set off.

With Romana missing on Bodcombe Moor he was genuinely worried. He had gone about half a mile across the moor, lost in grim thoughts about mineshafts and treacherous cliffs, when he tripped over K-9 coming in the other direction.

'Greetings, master,' said the robot.

'K-9,' complained the Doctor, rubbing a grazed knee, 'why can't you bark or something, so people will know you're there?'

'I am not programmed to bark, master.'

'Well, you should be. Still that's not your fault. I've got a job for you. You've always wanted to be a bloodhound, haven't you?'

'Negative, master.'

'No ambition – that's your trouble. I need you to find Romana. Can you do that?'

'I have a record of the mistress's scent, blood and tissue type, and her alpha wave patterns are recorded in my databank.'

'Then don't just talk about it, K-9. Do it!'

For a couple of minutes, K-9 swivelled in one direction, then another, and finally announced, 'The mistress is located this way.'

'Good dog,' declared the Doctor. 'Let's go and collect her.'

Together, Time Lord and robot crossed Bodcombe Moor to the cliff above Bodcombe Bay, and there they found Romana still huddled uncomfortably on her ledge. By now she was numb with both cold and fear.

'Mistress,' said K-9, peering over the edge.

Romana was delighted to hear him. 'K-9!' she called up. 'You can't imagine how pleased I am to see you.'

'Do not fear.' The automaton's tones were as neutral as ever. 'We shall rescue you. The master is here.'

'Oh no,' said Romana, 'not the Doctor.' She still retained a clear image of the tall familiar figure who had pushed her over the cliff.

At that moment the Doctor leaned over the cliff edge and dangled his long scarf down to Romana. 'Grab hold of this and I'll get you up in a jiffy.'

'No,' she cried bitterly. 'I'm not giving you a second chance to kill me.'

'Don't be absurd. Why would I want to kill you?'

'I don't know. But you've already tried once.'

The Doctor knew that shock could induce psychological trauma, so he decided to try and reason with her. 'Look here,' he said, 'if I was trying to kill you, I would have just left you, wouldn't I? I mean, it's only a matter of time before you topple into the briny down there.'

Romana considered this. He did have a point.

'Anyway,' he went on, 'this is no place for a serious discussion. Grab the scarf and I'll pull you up.'

Convinced by the logic of his argument, and by the reassuring presence of K-9, Romana reached for the scarf. Thanks to that and the few remaining bushes and handholds in the rock face, she climbed up to the lip of the cliff. The Doctor helped her over onto firm land, but once there she quickly scrabbled away from him.

'You pushed me over the cliff,' she insisted.

The Doctor was both shocked and hurt at the accusation. It didn't bode well for their mission to find the Key to Time. How could they operate as a team if she didn't trust him? The same thought had occurred to Romana. If the Doctor was sincere, then he deserved an explanation.

'While I was standing on the edge of the cliff,' she said, 'I heard someone laugh, and when I looked around I thought I saw you. And then someone pushed me over.'

'Well, it wasn't me.'

'Then it was something or someone that looked very much like you.'

'Did you see this figure clearly?'

'No,' admitted Romana, 'there was a very odd mist. But I didn't imagine it. It looked as solid as you do now.' She turned to K-9. 'Is this the real Doctor? Can you scan him to be sure?'

'You know very well that I am,' he told K-9. But, realising that if he was to convince Romana of the truth he had no alternative but to trust the little robot, he muttered, 'Oh, very well, go on.'

K-9 extended his facial antenna to make a full body scan of the figure in front of him. He then consulted his database, which contained everything about the Doctor, from his physical characteristics to his personal habits, including shoe and collar size and the structure of his genome. There was very little about the Doctor that K-9 did not know. He took his time about his cross-matching of the data, because he knew how important a definite identification was. But the result did not come fast enough for the Doctor, who vented his irritation at the delay.

'How long does it take?' he demanded. 'I think you need reprogramming.'

'Patience, master,' replied the robot. 'Please do not interrupt.'

Chastened, the Doctor waited until K-9 was ready to announce his conclusions.

'You are the Doctor,' he said, eventually.

'You're absolutely sure, K-9?' queried Romana, still unconvinced.

'Absolutely, mistress. Beyond doubt.'

Getting to her feet, she sighed and smiled a little sheepishly. 'You will understand I had to check.' When he said nothing, she asked, 'What do we do now?'

Accepting the unspoken apology, the Doctor declared, 'First, we stop off at the TARDIS to get you a decent pair of boots. Then we find who exactly did push you over the cliff.'

'Then we're looking for someone who looks exactly like you,' responded Romana.

He raised an eyebrow. 'Or someone with the power to transform their appearance.'

Romana started at the thought then nodded solemnly.

They both knew that just such a power was an intrinsic quality of the Key to Time.

Professor Rumford and Miss Fay were waiting in the stone circle for the return of the Doctor and Romana. Worried by their continued absence, the Professor was pacing up and down. It was good of Vivien to have come out looking for her. Emilia admired her calm as she sat nonchalantly on the altar stone, swinging her legs and trying to relieve her companion's distress.

'Emilia,' she said soothingly, 'I'm sure you're worrying needlessly. Neither the Doctor nor Romana struck me as fools. They'll be careful, I'm sure.'

'Well, I'm not,' replied the Professor. 'I should never have let him go off on his own, like that. Particularly in the dark. He doesn't know the Moor. You know how treacherous it can be. No, I ought to have gone after that girl myself.'

'Nonsense, Emilia. Someone had to stay behind in case she returned on her own.'

'Then it should have been him,' concluded the Professor. 'I should have argued it out with him.'

Miss Fay smiled to herself in the increasing darkness, imagining the clash. 'He looked to me like someone who was used to having his own way.'

'He's a man of science,' insisted the Professor. 'He would have seen the logic of my point of view.'

'But men can be such contrary creatures at times,' opined Miss Fay. 'Sometimes they simply can't be persuaded to see reason. And then what do you do?'

Not for the first time in their acquaintance, the Professor wondered about Vivien Fay's past. She really knew so very little about her. The woman had appeared one day out of nowhere, several years ago, when the Professor had begun her research into the Nine Travellers. The two of them had clicked immediately. Both were, it transpired, alumni of Somerville College, Oxford – though the Professor had to confess to some doubts about Vivien Fay on that score. Not long after they first met, the younger woman had referred to the head of the College as the Warden, whereas everyone who had actually studied there knew that the head was known as the Principal.

Perhaps more importantly, Vivien somehow didn't come across as a typical Somerville type. Clearly she had had some archaeological training. But it hadn't been under Professor Oakes, who had trained Emilia Rumford. Nevertheless, all such doubts had vanished when Vivien had revealed that she lived in a cottage nearby the stones and was thus able to provide a convenient base for Emilia's research. The Professor had accepted her offer and moved into Vivien Fay's spare bedroom the next day. It was like a prayer answered.

On a personal level, the Professor had learned that Miss Fay had been married at one time, but it had not worked out for some reason. The Professor was sympathetic. Her own relationships with men hadn't prospered over the years either. What was it about some men that they seemed unable to accept that an intelligent woman might have views and opinions of their own? And that they might be contrary to the man, or men, in her life? Why, she wondered, could they never accept that she was right and they were wrong? What was it about the male of the species that made them so pig-headed?

What's past is past, Emilia old girl, she told herself. You've no time for this nonsense. Your job now is to sort out the problem of the Nine Travellers. Still, it didn't stop her from worrying about the fate of poor Romana.

Fortunately, the Professor didn't have to wait much longer for her fears to be allayed. In fact, just as Miss Fay was telling the Professor, 'I wouldn't worry about the Doctor. I'm sure he can look after himself,' an answering voice came from beyond one of the perimeter stones:

'I wouldn't be too sure of that,' said Romana.

'Oh, thank heavens, you're safe, my girl,' declared the Professor, hugging Romana as if she'd been gone for days instead of a couple of hours. 'I was worried about you. Both of you,' she hastily added, as the Doctor appeared in tow. But then she saw K-9. 'What's that?' she exclaimed in something approaching horror.

'This is my dog,' explained the Doctor. 'He's called K-9.'

'But he's mechanical!'

'Affirmative,' agreed the little robot.

The Professor was taken aback. Something was wrong here, she felt. A mechanical dog: what was the world coming to? She turned to the Doctor in protest: 'Surely, isn't that rather . . . ?'

The Doctor waived aside her concerns. 'They're all

the rage in America, you know. They're manufactured in Trenton, New Jersey, where they also produce a range of robot cats and rabbits. Oh, and peacocks.'

'Peacocks?'

'I gather it's the latest must-have thing for anyone who lives in Beverley Hills.'

'Do you need a licence for it?' she asked, nodding in the direction of K-9.

'Negative,' rejoined the automaton.

'No,' the Doctor confirmed. 'At least not yet. But I'm sure the government will get around to taxing them sooner or later.' He liked to show off with his knowledge of Earth affairs.

Meanwhile, Romana had been busying herself with the Tracer, having decided to recheck the Circle. Suddenly she got a reaction – an electronic buzzing.

'What's that?' demanded Miss Fay, startled by the noise.

'Oh, just another little gadget,' replied the Doctor easily.

Romana was excited. 'It's here, Doctor,' she said. 'It's definitely here.'

'What is?' asked Miss Fay. 'What are you looking for?'

'Concentrations of radon,' replied the Doctor lightly. 'It plays havoc with K-9's systems.' Then, seeing that both Romana and K-9 were about to intervene, he turned to the Professor, 'Emilia, you've done a lot of research on this circle, haven't you?'

'Of course.'

'Legends? Folklore? History?'

'Nobody,' the Professor said stiffly, 'has ever had cause to question the quality of my research.'

'No, of course not,' replied the Doctor, attempting to soothe the indignant academic. 'I'm just trying to establish if you took notes of your research.'

'What's the point of doing any research,' demanded the Professor, 'if you don't record if? Of course I took notes! Copious notes. They're all back at Vivien's cottage.'

The Doctor beamed. 'Excellent. Then I presume you would have no objections to showing them to Romana. There are serious questions that remain to be answered about the Nine Travellers, as I'm sure you agree.'

'Indeed,' agreed the Professor. 'And I'd be delighted if Romana would like to go through my research material.'

Warming to his theme, the Doctor cajoled her further. 'With you at her elbow, of course.'

'Well,' murmured the Professor, 'if you think I can be of help . . .'

'Who else knows more about the circle than you, Professor? Certainly not Mr de Vries and his pathetic bunch of would-be druids.'

The Professor agreed wholeheartedly to showing Romana everything she had turned up about the Travellers and the mysterious goddess they were said to celebrate.

'Good,' said the Doctor. 'Then that's that.'

'What's *what?*' demanded Romana of him sotto voce. 'What are you going to be doing while I'm stuck with the Professor and Miss Fay?'

'Having a word with Mr de Vries.'

'But that's madness,' she protested. 'Look at what he nearly did to you.'

'That's precisely why I'm going to see him. I think by now Mr de Vries must be a very worried man – and worried men sing worried songs. Come on, K-9.'

And with that he swung on his heel and stalked out of the circle, taking the path to the manor.

'Sometimes I think he's quite mad,' said Romana, more to herself that the others.

'No. Just a typical man,' remarked Miss Fay. 'Opinionated. Hot-headed. Arrogant. And when you come down to it, not too bright.'

'That about sums him up,' agreed Romana, rather guiltily. After all, it was true that she had performed better than the Doctor at the Time Lord Academy.

The Professor, meanwhile, had reclaimed her ancient bike and was more interested in taking Romana through her notes at the cottage than in standing about bad-mouthing the Doctor. The fellow didn't seem so bad to her.

'Come on, girls,' she said, 'we haven't time to stand around. Back to the cottage. Pronto!' Then, turning to Romana, she added, 'There's a great deal to show you, my dear. Come on. Hop on the back.' She indicated the rear saddle basket.

Romana demurred. 'Do you mind if I just walk?' she asked.

'Nonsense. It will take forever and you might get lost again. No. no. Chop, chop.' She patted the rear saddle basket once again. 'Up you get! You might find it a bit uncomfortable at first, but what's a little discomfort when it comes to the Nine Travellers, eh?'

'It'll be a new experience for you,' joined in Miss Fay, wearing that disarming smile again. 'Nothing to be afraid of.'

The Professor switched on the lamp at the back of the bike and, with Romana on board and clutching desperately to her anorak, they wobbled away into the darkness, with Miss Fay following on her own sleek machine.

As the Doctor had predicted, back at Bodcombe Manor, Mr de Vries certainly was worried. And with good reason. He was trying to bring off a very tricky feat – placating an angry goddess. He was on his knees in the altar room, with his increasingly doubtful acolyte, Martha, kneeling beside him. How to assuage the anger of the Cailleach?

Martha's solution was simple. 'Let's just get in the car and go. We can be in Plymouth in a couple of hours.' Her brother had a flat on the Hoe, where she knew they could lie low for as long as they needed to.

But De Vries was not persuaded. 'For heaven's sake, Martha,' he said. 'Don't you understand? The Cailleach will find us wherever we run to. She's implacable.'

Martha was not prepared to give up so easily. 'But why should she be so unforgiving? You've served the Cailleach loyally in the past. You can't be blamed for one failure. I mean, it's one thing to be sacrificing chickens or even sheep – but humans! It's criminal. We could both end up in jail. And without us, who else would worship the Cailleach?'

It was certainly a thought, but De Vries was unconvinced. From what he knew of the Cailleach, benevolence and mercy were not in her vocabulary. She never forgave a slight, and was merciless in her revenge. Suddenly he realised something was missing from the room.

'Where's the bird?' he gasped.

The wooden perch where the raven usually sat was empty. The Cailleach's creature had left its place guarding the holy of holies. It had left them to their fate.

It was at this point that De Vries realised everything was lost. He and Martha were going to die. He prayed without hope: 'Great Goddess – Cailleach – I beg you to have mercy on your loyal servants.' But already he could hear the approach of something huge and heavy.

Martha heard it, too. 'What's that?' she shrieked.

De Vries had a sense of why Martha wouldn't leave and made a last effort to save his acolyte. 'Go,' he cried, 'get out now, Martha. There may still be time. Run as fast as you can!'

'No,' she replied. 'I'm not going to leave you. If we stay together . . .'

There was the sound of splintering wood as some monstrous creature smashed down the front door of the manor.

'Go,' screamed De Vries. 'Go!'

But it was already too late.

Chapter V

The Manor

The Doctor and K-9 heard loud crashes as they approached the manor. K-9 halted immediately, all his sensors fully deployed.

'Caution, master, danger. Unidentified aliens ahead. Species unknown.'

'That's helpful, I must say,' the Doctor grumbled. 'Can't you do better than that, K-9?' When there was no reply from the robot, the Doctor tried a different tack. 'Do you know where they are now?'

'In the manor, master.'

'I suppose it's just possible that this Cailleach herself has decided to call in person. In which case, perhaps we ought to extend a talon in welcome.' Then the Doctor heard sounds of further destruction from the manor followed by screams suddenly cut short. 'Come on, K-9!' he hissed as he ran up the drive to the old house, followed by his robotic companion.

They came upon a scene of utter destruction. The heavy oak doors of the manor were splintered to matchwood and scattered on the ground. Indeed, the whole facade of the building looked as if a battle tank had entered via the front door.

Cautiously, the Doctor picked his way through the rubble until he came upon the horrific sight of two corpses, barely recognisable as De Vries and Martha. They looked as if they had been run over by a huge truck. Their once white robes were now heavily blood-stained. They were clearly very dead.

'Poor devils,' said the Doctor. 'Crushed to death. It's the kind of thing that could put you off the Cailleach for good.'

K-9 had detected something else amongst the bloody mayhem in the manor. A greyish powder lay scattered amongst the carnage and rubble. He sniffed at it inquisitively, in a remarkable impression of a real dog. 'Silicon, master.'

'I wonder where that came from?' mused the Doctor.

'From whatever creature attacked the two humans. There is a trail. It leads through here.' K-9 moved into the altar room, eager to trace the unknown creature.

'Steady, old chap,' warned the Doctor. 'Don't get carried away. We don't know what we're dealing with yet.'

Whatever it was had passed through the altar room like a fifty-tonne truck, leaving a further trail of destruction and grey silicon dust everywhere. The Doctor cautiously followed. He walked up to the gaping hole where the French windows had been and peered out into the night.

'It seems all clear now. Whatever did this must have gone.'

'Negative,' exclaimed K-9. 'Caution, master.'

Suddenly the creature, which had been lurking in the shadows of the room, lunged in the direction of the Doctor, showering him with broken glass and brick dust. He tripped and fell to the floor. He was not seriously hurt, but now lay at the mercy of the creature. As it moved to crush him, exactly as it had crushed De Vries and Martha, K-9 sprang into action. He brought his weaponry into play and fired an electronic beam at the thing standing over the Doctor.

For a moment the creature was irradiated by an intense blue light. K-9 had scored a direct hit. A weird scream of pain rang out, as some part of the entity crumbled and fell to the floor. The thing turned and lumbered off into the darkness – with K-9 in full pursuit.

'No! Come back, K-9!' yelled the Doctor. But for once the little robot, now in full battle mode, ignored its master. It was determined to track and identify the creature.

The Doctor paused for a moment to see what had fallen off his attacker. But on inspection it turned out to be a piece of stone, a metre and a half in length and about a metre thick. Was it a weapon of some kind? Or part of the strange creature itself? There was no way of telling.

And in any case a more important task lay ahead – the recall of K-9 before he clashed again with this attacker. The Doctor knew his dog had powerful defences, but just from the sheer size of the creature he suspected that K-9 would have to call upon all his reserves to avoid serious damage in their next encounter.

Meanwhile, back at Miss Fay's cottage, Romana was busy. True to her promise, Professor Rumford had brought out all her research material on the Nine Travellers. Truly it was an embarrassment of riches – box files and thick cardboard folders bulging with papers, all of them needing to be studied. There was so much material that at first Romana had barely known where to begin, but now she was at last making headway.

The entrance of the Professor, with steaming mugs of tea, came as a welcome relief. 'How are you getting on, my dear?' she asked, handing one of the mugs over.

'I've made a start at least,' replied Romana. 'I'm just amazed at the amount of material you've managed to collect.'

'If you're going to research something, you might as well do it properly, that's what I always say,' affirmed the Professor. 'Vivien's on kitchen duty making sausage sandwiches. Nothing like a sausage sandwich to stimulate the brain. You'd like a couple, of course.'

Romana nodded, rather unhappily. She sometimes found the Professor's ebullience overwhelming. Sausage sandwiches were not one of the culinary delights the Doctor had mentioned. He had told her, though, that one of the hazards with interplanetary travel was that, out of common courtesy, you were expected to eat things you normally wouldn't touch with a multi-fortescope.

Taking a break, and a few sips of sweet tea, Romana felt herself warming to this elderly scholar. 'What about your family, Professor?' she enquired. 'Are they all academics too?'

'Heavens, no,' came the reply. 'The Rumfords are a military lot. Brawn, my dear, not brains. My eldest brother, Hector, who was a colonel in the Sappers – or whatever they call them nowadays – got himself blown up, poor darling, trying to defuse a bomb in Northern Ireland. My youngest brother, Jasper, is the fool of the family. He went into the Church; Sandhurst wouldn't have him.'

Romana wasn't sure if this was good or not. Tentatively she said, 'You must be very proud of him.'

'Why?' demanded the Professor. 'Jasper spends most of his time trying to keep out of the Sunday newspapers. He tends to confuse Karl Marx with Matins. The boy's an idiot, my dear . . .' She indicated the pile of research material: 'Any questions so far?'

Only too glad to return to safe ground, Romana nodded. 'Just one. You identify our Nine Travellers, our stone circle, as one of the Three Gorsedds of Prophecy. What's a gorsedd?'

'Old Welsh,' said the Professor. 'A gorsedd is a place of augurs. People who foretell the future. There's an ancient Welsh triad that explains it. You'll find it in my notes.'

Miss Fay entered at that moment, bearing a plate of sandwiches before her. Hearing Romana's questions she recited the triad: 'The three gorsedds in the isle of Britain are the gorsedd of Salisbury in England—'

'That's Stonehenge, of course,' interjected the Professor.

'. . . the gorsedd of Bryn Gwyddon in Wales, and the gorsedd of Bodcombe Moor in Damnonium.'

'That's our Nine Travellers,' Emilia explained.

'But why should this particular circle become a place of prophecy?' asked Romana. 'You said yourself that there are a dozen or more stone circles in this part of the country, many of them bigger than the Nine Travellers. Why not one of them?'

'If I knew that, girl,' replied the Professor, 'I'd be Professor of Megalithic Archaeology at Bangor and not that fool Hugh Morgan. I'm hoping that you'll find something out amongst this lot –' she indicated the intimidating pile of research papers on the table – 'that answers the question. Why here and not somewhere else? I'd dearly like to know.'

She reached for a sausage sandwich and smiled encouragingly at Romana. 'Anything you come up with, anything that strikes you – I'm eager to hear it.'

'There is one thing that does strike me as curious,' observed Romana.

'What?' enquired Miss Fay.

Romana reached for one of the files and leafed through its contents. 'Well,' she went on, 'until recently the land which the circle stands on has always been owned by a woman. Haven't you noticed? Lady Montcalm, Mrs Trefusis, Senhora Camara, and if you go further back, in the Middle Ages it came under the control of the mother superior of the convent of the Little Sisters of St Gudula.'

'Interesting woman, St Gudula,' agreed the Professor, munching away on her sandwich. 'Born some time between 710 and 715 in Brabant. She's the patron saint of Brussels, I believe. The poor woman was much afflicted by demons, they say. Kept blowing out her candle whilst she was reading the Bible at night.'

But Miss Fay was not impressed. 'For heaven's sake,' she said, 'lots of convents owned enormous areas of land in the Middle Ages. There's every reason for a mother superior to be a landowner. She was the representative of her order, after all: the managing director of the company, you might say.'

Romana shook her head. 'But it happens over such a long period of time – from the eleventh century to the early 1800s. That's seven or eight hundred years without a single male owner.'

'What are you suggesting?' demanded Miss Fay.

'Some kind of sisterhood that's been worshipping these stones since the year dot?'

'What other explanation is there?'

Miss Fay paused, then tried another tack. 'So how does Mr de Vries play a role in all this? He doesn't qualify as the head of the sisterhood.'

Romana had to admit that Miss Fay had a point. From what she'd heard of Mr de Vries, he did not strike her as a natural leader of women – or men, come to that. 'What about that convent of the Little Sisters, does it still exist?'

'Good heavens, no,' replied the Professor. 'It was abolished by Henry VIII in the Dissolution of the Monasteries. Typical piece of male chauvinism, if you ask me.'

But Romana had the bit between her teeth. 'What happened to the convent records?'

'Destroyed long ago,' declared Miss Fay.

This time the Professor wasn't so sure. 'I don't know about that,' she said. 'The authorities at the time will have needed them to establish the extent of the convent's lands. If the records still exist – and I don't say that they do – they could be somewhere at the manor.'

'Let's go and take a look,' proposed Romana. 'What are we waiting for?'

Always ready for action, the Professor leapt to her feet and clapped her hands. 'Good girl! That's the spirit I like. No time like the present. Up and at 'em, eh? Get my bike, Vivien.' She turned to Romana. 'You can ride on the back again.'

Romana blanched at the prospect of another nightmarish ride across moorland in the dark, perched on the back of the Professor's old boneshaker.

Fortunately, Miss Fay came to the rescue. 'Romana can borrow my bicycle,' she said. 'You don't need me with you, do you, Emilia?'

The Professor was busy searching through drawers in an old Welsh dresser. 'No,' she agreed. In the time she had been living at Miss Fay's cottage, she had come to treat the place like her own. 'You keep a good fire burning here in case the Doctor gets back before us.'

'You'll be better off on my bike,' Miss Fay murmured to Romana. 'It's got a comfortable saddle and the brakes work. Emilia shouldn't be allowed to ride around the countryside on that old machine of hers. Belonged to her father, you know.'

Romana quietly thanked her. The only problem she now envisaged was learning to ride the thing.

'Found it!' exclaimed the Professor, producing a large wooden club from the dresser drawer.

'What's that?' Romana asked.

'A policeman's truncheon,' Miss Fay informed her. 'She took it with her when she went to a lecture in New York last year – in case she got mugged.'

Not knowing what getting mugged meant, Romana involuntarily asked, 'And did she?'

'No,' mused Miss Fay. 'She got arrested for carrying an offensive weapon.'

'Come on, Romana,' boomed the Professor, opening the cottage door. 'Tally-ho!'

Having observed only once how it was done, Romana learnt to keep her balance on the bicycle surprisingly quickly. Even so, she found it impossible to go as fast as the Professor, who shouted over and over, 'Keep up girl! Keep up!' while the lights on her bike threatened to disappear in the distance.

When Romana eventually arrived at the manor, she found the Professor examining the damaged entrance. 'Good grief,' she said. 'Was there an explosion? Did a bomb go off?'

'No, I don't think so,' replied Emilia. 'No scorch marks. No smell of burning. It looks to me as if something very big and powerful was determined to get in.'

They stepped over the rubble and entered the manor, following the trail of devastation to the altar room, where they found the Doctor crouched over a battered K-9. Romana hurried over to them.

'Oh, K-9, what have they done to you?'

'Poor little fellow,' sympathised the Professor. 'Is he badly hurt?'

The Doctor prised open an inspection panel in the side of the robot. 'We'll know in a moment,' he said.

At last, K-9 spoke. His voice was very weak. The Doctor leant closer to hear him.

'I did my best, master,' whispered the automaton. 'But it was so strong . . .'

'What was it?' asked the Doctor.

'A silicon life form . . . globulin deficient. Physiognomy suggests origins in . . .' The voice ran down into an unintelligible mumble.

The Doctor was excited by K-9's description. 'Globulin deficient. I knew it!'

'But is K-9 all right?' demanded Romana.

The Doctor shook his head. 'He's expended too much energy. His circuitry is nearly all burned out.'

She lowered her voice, circumspectly. 'But it is repairable?'

His hearing clearly unimpaired, K-9 interjected his own opinion. 'Initial damage reports suggest not, mistress. Advise cannibalisation of any reusable parts.'

The Doctor cheerfully disagreed. 'Nonsense, K-9. We're not going to turn you into scrap yet. Are we, Romana?' He took her arm and led her to one side.

'But what can we do?' she asked.

The Doctor put his hand to his head. What could he tell her? Common sense said that K-9 ought to be cannibalised. But they were both inordinately fond of the loveable computer.

'K-9's only chance,' he said finally, 'is total circuit

regeneration. But how do we do that in time to save him? Perhaps the kindest thing we can do is to remove the cerebral cortex now . . .'

Romana was appalled. K-9 had been dedicated to their safety for so long that he deserved better of them. 'If we remove the cerebral cortex,' she pointed out, 'he's finished. We can't do that.'

'What do you suggest?'

She considered, then spoke. 'Is the TARDIS fitted with a molecular stabiliser?'

'Yes, of course,' he replied. 'All Type Forties were.'

'I thought so. We had a lecture once at the Academy on the latest techniques for circuitry regeneration. If we link the molecular stabiliser through the circuit frequency modulators . . .'

'Brilliant!' exclaimed the Doctor, his voice ringing through the hall like a gunshot.

'Do you really think so?'

'No. But it's worth a try anyway.'

'We have to do something,' Romana pointed out. 'Look at him. He's on his last legs.'

'All right,' said the Doctor. 'Take the poor little chap back to the TARDIS and connect him to the modulator.'

Romana picked up K-9 and prepared to leave. 'What will you do?' she asked.

'Oh, Professor Rumford and I will look at the bodies.'

'What bodies?' demanded the Professor, who had been lurking respectfully in the background.

'De Vries and the woman,' explained the Doctor. 'They're dead. Killed by that creature. The one K-9 described as globulin deficient.'

'What does that mean?' enquired the Professor, assimilating the news with academic stoicism.

The Doctor elaborated. 'Globulin is a protein found in blood plasma. The creature that killed them lives on blood.'

'Like a vampire?'

'Good grief, no!' declared the Doctor. 'Poor old Bram Stoker got it all wrong. And he certainly had no knowledge of dentistry. I mean, think about it. All that indiscriminate biting. No time to clean your teeth properly between meals. Blood everywhere. Talk about halitosis. A vampire's breath must have been lethal at twenty paces.'

Romana and the Professor exchanged a glance, wondering where this particular tangent was leading.

'No, Professor,' the Doctor finally concluded. 'We won't find Dracula hanging round the manor. But I strongly suspect we may find something equally disturbing.'

Back in the stone circle, preparations were already well under way for a fresh blood sacrifice to the Cailleach. Unbeknownst to the Doctor, the bodies of De Vries and Martha had already been spirited away from the manor and placed on the altar stone. Bending over them now crouched a nightmarish figure wearing a feather cloak and a bird mask – the Cailleach herself.

She was draining the two corpses of blood, which she gathered in an ornate bronze bowl. When the task was complete, the goddess rose and placed the bowl on the altar. She patted the foot of the dead De Vries and said almost cheerfully: 'There you are, Anton. What did I tell you? Even in death you can be of use to the Cailleach. The Ogri will be most grateful for your contributions to their welfare.'

She took up the bowl, crossed to one of the stones, and poured the blood over it. As the scarlet liquid streamed over the stone, something extraordinary occurred. The stone absorbed it. It drank the blood. In the depths of the stone, light flickered. There followed the sound of a slow, heavy, muffled heartbeat – as if the stone were coming to life.

In the library of the manor, the Professor was busy going through books on the shelves when the Doctor entered. The disappearance of the two bodies had been noted but, as he had told her, they had other fish to fry.

'Found anything?' he asked.

'Nothing prior to 1700. Otherwise what's here is pretty much a load of rubbish. Lots of stories about Lady Montcalm, who does seem to have been a particularly nasty piece of work. But nothing that tells us anything useful. How about you?'

'Nothing. I've searched the whole house. No secret passage. No hidden rooms. But it's got to be here somewhere.'

'What has?' enquired the Professor.

'The Cailleach, of course.'

The Professor was surprised. She would never have believed that the Doctor was superstitious. 'But that's just a legend,' she protested. 'The Witch Hag. The Greek Sphinx. The Demon of Death. The Etruscan Alpan. She's had many names, but she's still only a legend.'

'So was Troy,' pointed out the Doctor, 'until dear old Schliemann dug it up. But legends often have a habit of turning into reality. So where is she? Morrigu. Morridwyn. In five thousand years, bet she's gone through quite a few names. Yet there are no statues of her here, no images, no paintings . . .' A thought struck him. 'The missing pictures. They *must* be here somewhere.'

The Professor was beginning to lose patience with the Doctor. Creatures that drank blood? Welsh goddesses? And now he was in search of some missing pictures! Steady on, old girl, she told herself. He's just a man, and they're never the most stable or sensible of creatures . . .

But the Doctor was following his own train of thought. 'Why have the paintings been hidden?' he demanded. 'There must be a reason. And more to the point, where are they?'

Then it came to him – birds! Beware the raven and the crow – that's what De Vries had said. And where had he seen the raven and the crow?

'Come on,' he said to the Professor, taking her by the arm and half-dragging her to the altar room.

'What are we looking for?' she demanded.

'Birds, Emilia! Birds!'

And there they were – a series of carved figures over the room's vast seventeenth-century fireplace. Raven. Crow. Rook. Falcon. Eagle. Idly, he ran his hands over the carvings, and as he did so one moved. In response, a concealed door in the back of the fireplace opened.

'Jumping Joshua!' cried the Professor. 'A priest hole! In everything I've read about Bodcombe Manor, I don't recall any mention of a priest hole.'

The Doctor didn't wait to discuss historical details. Instead, he ducked his head to avoid a massive oak cross beam and stepped through the fireplace into the narrow passageway beyond. It was dark and smelt musty.

'Careful, Emilia,' he said to the Professor, who was following close behind. 'Do you have a light?'

'I don't smoke, Doctor. I suppose there might be some firelighters . . .'

'No time for that. Stay close behind me and look out for a light switch.'

Both proceeded to feel their way in the darkness. The passage began to slope downwards and widen at the same time.

'I think we're coming to the end of it,' said the Doctor after a while. He stepped out with his left foot and encountered only air. Fortunately, at that moment Professor Rumford located an electric light switch, the flicking of which revealed the Doctor to be wobbling at the top of a flight of steps. He hung on to both sides of the passage and heaved a sigh of relief.

'Thank you, Emilia.'

The steps led down into a large cavern. It was clearly a natural feature, though it had been further enlarged at some time in the past. Even with the solitary naked lightbulb hanging overhead, the far end was shrouded in darkness. The Doctor gained the hazy impression of several other passageways leading off.

Propped up against the walls of the cavern were three oil paintings. The Professor's first thought was that De Vries had been a philistine, and that such precious antiques ought to be properly protected from the dank atmosphere. Then she studied them more closely.

Each one was a portrait of a woman.

'Good grief!' the Professor cried. 'I don't believe it.'

'I do,' declared the Doctor. 'It's the only explanation that makes sense. Look . . .' He took each painting in turn and held it up to the light. 'Meet the wicked Lady Montcalm . . . then Mrs Trefusis, the lonely recluse . . .

and, last but not least, Senhora Camara, the Brazilian lady who built the alms houses in Bodcombe Parva.'

Professor Rumford's mind was racing to keep up with the evidence of her eyes. 'But they all look like the same person.'

'That's because they are,' the Doctor agreed.

'And I seem to know that face.'

The Doctor nodded, and patted the old academic kindly on her shoulder. 'So you should,' he went on. 'It's the face of your friend, Vivien Fay!'

The Professor stared at him, aghast.

Having left K-9 rigged up to the molecular stabiliser in the TARDIS, Romana was now making her way back across the moor to Bodcombe Manor. The route took her past the Nine Travellers, and suddenly she stopped in her tracks. Ahead of her she could see a weird glow that seemed to emanate from within the stone circle. It was a striking sight in the otherwise pitch-black night. Intrigued, she began to run towards it, when out of the darkness a hand seized her arm. She screamed in alarm. But it was only Miss Fay, who was carrying an illuminated staff of some kind.

'You scared the life out of me!' said Romana.

'Did I? Sorry,' purred Miss Fay. 'There's something going on in the circle. I don't know what, but I think we should take a look.'

Gently, she led Romana into the circle of stones,

where the ground itself was lit by the phosphorescent glow. An odd humming noise seemed to grow louder as they approached the altar stone. Instinctively knowing that something was wrong, Romana tried to pull back, but a push from Miss Fay sent her staggering into the centre of the circle.

'What's going on?' demanded Romana. 'What are you doing to me?'

Miss Fay took her staff and drew a ring around them both in the grass. Wherever the staff touched, it burned, surrounding them with a circle of smoking turf.

'You can't run away now,' she announced. 'You're inside a force field. If you touch it, you'll burn yourself quite badly. In any case, after we've made the leap into hyperspace, you'll feel quite ill for a while and you won't have the strength to do anything silly.'

Before Romana could reply, she became aware of a strange sensation, as if she was being pushed, bit by bit, down an ever-narrowing tunnel. It hurt, and she screamed. Left shaking and feeling sick, it didn't help that, while she was trying to recover, Miss Fay prodded her firmly with her staff. The pain was indescribable. The floor, which suddenly seemed to be made of metal, rose up and struck her. She became aware of dust lying everywhere, and an empty, echoing space. Everything went black.

Her last thought was that Vivien Fay had placed her in a metal tomb.

*

In the cavern beneath the manor, Professor Rumford was studying the portraits. 'I suppose Vivien could be related to the Montcalm family,' she said. 'Though she never mentioned it to me.'

'More than related,' declared the Doctor. 'She *is* the Montcalm family. The wicked Lady Montcalm, at least. And the Trefusis family, too. Ever wondered why Mrs Trefusis lived like a recluse, seeing nobody? It was because she was terrified someone would recognise her. When it came to Senhora Camara, she could relax. Who was alive then to recognise the infamous Lady Montcalm? I daresay she enjoyed being the great lady bountiful – building alms houses and installing stained-glass windows in the local church. I wouldn't mind betting she has links to the land-management company that owns the circle today.'

'And influence over the local council, stopping the National Trust from taking over,' the Professor reasoned. 'But look at the dates! Vivien would have had to have been around for two hundred and fifty years at least!'

'What's two hundred and fifty years when you've been here for more than four thousand? Don't you understand Emilia, your friend Vivien Fay *is* the Cailleach! The Witch Hag, Morrigu, Morridwyn and the rest of them – she's masqueraded as them all.'

'But why? Why is she here?'

'That, my dear, Emilia,' said the Doctor, 'is what we have to find out.'

They heard a noise behind them, and turned to find a huge, glowing, grey stone-like creature emerging from the far end of the cavern.

'What is that?' the Professor asked nervously.

'You heard K-9. A silicon-based life form. It looks rather like one of your Nine Travellers out for a dance.' The Doctor grinned unexpectedly. 'That would explain the legends! Rather restores your faith in people's ability to count, doesn't it?'

'Possibly,' the Professor conceded, in shock. 'What do we do now?'

'Run!'

Chapter VI

Joselito

'Come on!' yelled the Doctor. 'Do keep up!'

The Professor muttered something uncomplimentary about men, but managed to increase her speed, as they fled from the strange stone creature along one of the passages which led off the cavern. To their mutual surprise, it rose into a decrepit greenhouse in the old kitchen garden, where they paused to catch their breath. The night air smelt wonderful after the damp, musty cavern.

Panting heavily, the Professor leaned against the wall of the kitchen garden. 'I never thought we'd get out of there alive,' she gasped. 'I'm not used to this kind of thing. In archaeology you don't usually have to run a lot, you know. Particularly from the very things you're studying.'

'We're not clear, yet,' warned the Doctor. 'We can't stop now. Keep going.' In the rather forlorn hope of holding up their pursuer, he shut the garden gate behind them and jammed a wheelbarrow against it.

By now the Professor had had time to think and

wanted some questions answered. 'Did I understand you correctly?' she demanded. 'We're being pursued by a monolith – or something very like one?'

The ancient greenhouse suddenly exploded as the stone monstrosity emerged from the underground passage.

'Yes,' replied the Doctor. 'And in case you hadn't noticed, it's closing on us fast.'

'But that's impossible.'

'No, it isn't,' he pointed out. 'We're standing still while *it's* going like the clappers.' He seized her hand. 'Run!' And they set off for open land.

'What I meant,' she persisted, breaking into a very creditable trot for a woman in her sixties, 'was that a silicon-based life form is biologically unheard of ... unknown ... impossible ... It just can't be.'

As the Doctor looked back, he saw the creature reduce the garden gate and wheelbarrow to splinters. 'Maybe it doesn't know that,' he observed. 'Can you run any faster, Emilia?'

The Professor did her best. But her curiosity soon overcame her fear. 'Doctor,' she panted, 'don't you think that in the cause of science it is our duty to capture that creature? A silicon-based life form. Think what the Royal Society would make of that.'

'Think what *it'll* make of *us* if it catches us!'

'I'm serious,' insisted Emilia Rumford. 'If it doesn't belong to the circle we ought to track it to its lair.'

'And then what? Hit it over the head with our shoes?'

The Professor did not reply. She held up her hand. 'Ssh! Hear that? It's the sea. We must be near the cliffs.'

'Good,' he replied. 'Just keep going.' He kept glancing over his shoulder. When they reached the cliff edge and he could hear the waves thundering against the rocks below, he stopped and began to take off his coat. This was very close to where he had rescued Romana.

'What are you doing, Doctor?' demanded the Professor, appalled. 'I know you're under strain but jumping off a cliff isn't going to help. You'll be killed on the rocks.'

The Doctor moved up to the creature and waved his coat in its face, like a bullfighter trying to persuade the bull to charge.

'Hey, *toro*, *toro*!' he shouted.

Now almost upon them, the stone creature came at the Doctor like an express train. But the latter stepped easily to one side and swung his coat, going down on one knee as he did so. Following the coat instead, the creature hurtled over the cliff. It plummeted, mute and helpless, through the air until it shattered on the sea-lashed rocks fifty metres below.

The two brave survivors of the encounter peered over the cliff edge. On the thin shore lay a large pile of boulders lit by a brief glow, but then the sea washed over them and the glow was extinguished.

'I think it's a goner,' observed the Doctor.

'Pity,' sighed the Professor. 'The first silicon-based life form on Earth. What a loss to science.'

'Better than the loss of a distinguished professor of archaeology, don't you think?'

'I suppose so,' she replied. Then, ever curious, she enquired, 'What was that thing you did with your coat?'

'Oh, you mean the veronica. Just one of the moves matadors use in bullfighting. I learned it years ago from a *torero* I knew in Seville. Joselito. Probably one of the greatest matadors who ever lived. Lovely fellow. Very brave. Always worked very close to the bull. Trouble was he adored his food and one day he found he was so fat he couldn't get out of the way of the beast when it charged. Terrible tragedy.'

The Professor didn't approve of bullfighting, but under the circumstances felt she could hardly complain about the Doctor's expertise, so she tutted sympathetically and peered over the cliff edge once more. 'I suppose it really is dead?'

'Joselito?'

'The stone.'

'Oh, I think so,' he replied. 'Want to go down and find out?'

'I'd rather go and find Romana,' said the Professor.

But instead of Romana they found the Cailleach in the circle: a sinister figure in bird mask and feathered cloak.

Before they could approach her, she hastily drew a circle in the turf around her feet with her staff. Wherever the staff touched the grass it left a smouldering trail.

'No need to wear a mask now, Miss Fay,' said the Doctor. 'We know who you are.'

'That's a relief,' the Cailleach replied mildly and removed the offending article. Miss Fay smiled and wiped her brow. 'You don't know how tired I am of disguises. Never able to relax for a minute.'

Professor Rumford could only stare. 'Vivien, he says you're the Cailleach.'

'My dear, I've been so many things over so many years sometimes I find it hard to remember who I really am.'

'Still, I wish you had told me,' said the Professor, rather as if she had discovered her friend was a vegetarian. 'I'm sure we could have worked something out.'

'I can't think which I find more irritating about you, Emilia – your eternal enthusiasm for that godforsaken circle or your puerile optimism that everything will work out for the best. It doesn't. It never has. And it never will.'

'Since you raised the question yourself, Miss Fay,' the Doctor interjected, 'who are you? I assume you became Miss Fay, Somerville graduate, shortly before you met the Professor. But going back much further, long before the Cailleach, what was your name? And where were you from?'

Miss Fay ignored the question.

'Give it up, Vivien,' said the Professor kindly. 'Can't you see it's all finished now?'

'Not while I hold the trump card, Emilia.'

'And what is that?' asked the Doctor.

'Romana.'

The Doctor looked around. 'Romana!' he called into the night air. 'Romana!' Then, turning to Miss Fay, he demanded, 'What have you done with her? Where is she?'

'Where you'll never find her,' she smiled. 'Romana's perfectly safe so long as you leave me in peace.'

'I can't do that,' he said, advancing on her.

'Don't come any closer.'

The Doctor ignored her. He put out his hand to take her arm, but encountered something that burned him and caused him to be hurled to the ground. He sat up slowly and blew on the palm of his hand, which felt as if he had tried to hold a hot iron. 'Static electrical charge. Bit primitive,' he observed.

'Very efficient, though.'

Ruefully rubbing his scorched hand, the Doctor was forced to agree – primitive and painful.

'Don't worry about Romana,' Miss Fay went on. 'She's safe for the time being.'

'Why don't I believe you?'

'I'd worry about your own safety if I were you. I'm sure Romana can look after herself.'

She waved in the direction of the stones, three of which he now saw were missing. 'Count the stones, Doctor. Beware the Ogri!'

With that she disappeared in a flash of light.

The Doctor gingerly reached out a hand to where the Cailleach had been standing and found that the force field had vanished along with its creator. Only a ring of charred turf remained where once it had been.

'What did she mean about the stones?' demanded the Professor. 'What's happened to them?'

'One went over the cliff, Emilia. Don't you remember? And the whereabouts of the other two are a matter of some concern. The last thing we want is to have any more Ogri hunting us across the moor.'

'Ogri?' queried the Professor. 'What's an Ogri?'

'Your genuine silicon-based life form. I had my suspicions, but Miss Fay has just confirmed them. At least three of the Nine Travellers are Ogri.'

'I've never heard of them.'

'I'm not surprised,' replied the Doctor. 'They're normally found on their home planet Ogros, in Tau Ceti. Horrible place, nothing but mud and swamps of amino acids. Melts your boots as soon as you set foot there. But the Ogri love it. They can feed by sitting in all that goo and absorbing the amino acids and any other goodies that come along. Including other Ogri, of course.'

Professor Rumford gawped. 'They're cannibals then?'

'Luckily, or else the galaxy would be overrun by them. Here, on Earth, they feed on blood. Human or animal. I don't imagine they're too fussy, which is why Vivien Fay had to stay here for thousands of years organising blood sacrifices on the stones. Otherwise, she wouldn't be able to control them.'

When the Professor thought of carnivorous, blood-sucking monoliths roaming around the West Country, her own blood ran cold. A few hundred Ogri could devastate the entire country in no time. A few hundred thousand could devastate a continent.

'But what is Vivien doing with these things in the first place? And what are they doing here?'

'I don't know,' admitted the Doctor. 'But we're going to find out.'

The Professor clapped her hands approvingly. 'That's the ticket,' she said. 'Up and at 'em. I like that.' But then a thought struck her. 'Shouldn't we be armed, Doctor?'

He shook his head. 'Short of field artillery, I can't think of anything that could stop an Ogri.'

'You did,' she said.

'Thanks to Joselito and a steep cliff. Next time we might meet one that understands bullfighting.'

They stood for a while, with only the wind and the call of a lonely owl to punctuate the silence. Eventually the Professor asked, 'Is there anything I can do?'

The Doctor's reply was low and brooding. 'Yes. Find me some tritium crystals.'

She stared at him blankly. 'What are they? And where am I going to find them?'

'If I'm right,' said the Doctor, 'they'll be somewhere in Miss Fay's cottage. They're green, the colour of emeralds, and about the size of your thumbnail.'

'Suppose she hasn't got any?'

'Oh, she's bound to have tritium crystals somewhere around – they power that staff of hers. You go to the cottage and search everywhere, while I go back to the TARDIS and get some equipment.' Then, with a dramatic gesture, he went on: 'Off you go, Emilia. Hurry!'

He watched the Professor mount her trusty boneshaker, switch on her bicycle lamps and pedal off into the darkness. Her voice floated back to him over the heather: 'You can rely on me, Doctor!'

Chapter VII

A Theoretical Absurdity

When the Professor parked her old bicycle outside Miss Fay's cottage, she sighed with relief. Back safe and sound. No sign of those awful Ogri – not yet, at any rate. When she let herself into the cottage, however, she felt distinctly uneasy. After all, she had lived here for months, paying her whack, of course, but she had come to think of Vivien Fay as a friend. And Emilia Rumford valued friendship highly. What she was doing now made her feel like a burglar, which was silly, she conceded, because she had a key. But it still didn't feel right.

Come on, old girl, she told herself. Don't go soft now. The Doctor and Romana are relying on you. Time to get your skates on and find these blasted crystals – if they do exist!

It was then, as she looked around the familiar surroundings of the cottage, that the enormity of her task struck home. Where could you hide tritium crystals – whatever they might be – in a small country cottage on

Bodcombe Moor? Where do I start, she wondered? What if I can't find them?

Be positive, she told herself. Don't give way to defeatism. She decided that the best way to search the cottage was to treat it as an ancient tomb. An archaeological site that hid some precious artefact. The trick, as someone she knew who had successfully excavated ancient Mayan sites in Central America had told her, was to learn to think like the Maya. In this case, think like Vivien Fay.

Where would Vivien hide something that must have been vital to her wellbeing here on Earth? In the garden? No, she decided. Vivien had never shown the slightest interest in horticulture ever since she had known her. Besides, you couldn't be sure that your cache would remain undiscovered. Rabbits, badgers, stray dogs and inquisitive children might dig it up at any time. Moreover, if the crystals were that important to you, you would want to keep them close at hand. Therefore, logic decreed that they must be somewhere inside the cottage, and easily available.

Professor Rumford began in Vivien's bedroom. It might have been the logical place to start, but it made her feel more like a burglar than ever. She searched through the various drawers of the dressing table, and even went to the extent of feeling in the pockets of the clothes hanging in the wardrobe. She did not find any crystals, but she did find a jewel box. She had always admired Vivien's jewellery – particularly that heavy quartz pendant she always wore, which unsurprisingly was absent from the box. That was some sort of modern piece, whereas her other jewellery here was clearly much older. No wonder, she thought, if the Doctor's right about Vivien's past. The wicked Lady Montcalm must have amassed quite a lot of trinkets in the course of her eventful life – but, as soon became clear, she didn't keep them with her tritium crystals.

Where to look next? What had Vivien been interested in, Emilia asked herself? Cooking (she was an excellent cook), tapestry (she always seemed to have a piece of *petit point* on the go), and watercolours (at which she was also highly proficient). The Professor considered the options. Could one sew crystals into a tapestry? Too difficult, she thought. Somehow you would have to stitch them into the design itself – and suppose they popped out? Come to that, where could you hide a handful of crystals in a watercolour? Possibly inside an ornate frame. But none of the pictures in the cottage could boast such a thing.

That seemed to leave the kitchen as the favoured option. A place where, as the Professor quickly realised, there were almost too many potential hiding places. Nonetheless she attacked the room with the ferocity of a buccaneer ransacking a treasure ship. No quarter given, and she never stopped for a breather. The kitchen sink was soon full of flour, sugar, oatmeal, powdered coconut and the contents of the spice cupboard.

When the Doctor eventually returned to the cottage with K-9 at his heels, he found Professor Rumford standing in the kitchen covered in flour and investigating a jar of pickled onions with a knitting needle. 'Cooking something nice?' he asked.

The Professor triumphantly peeled the pickled onion to reveal a green tritium crystal hidden inside. 'I couldn't understand why Vivien had a jar of pickled onions when neither of us like them,' she said. 'So I investigated.' She indicated a small pile of similar jewels she had collected on the draining board. 'Any good?'

'Smart work, Emilia.'

'What's that you've got?' she asked.

The Doctor was weighed down with a bizarre piece of equipment. It had a huge wire cone at one end and a mass of circuitry at the other. 'Oh, just a little something I knocked together,' he replied. 'Pass me a crystal, would you?' After studying each one carefully, the Doctor nodded and began inserting them into the equipment he had built.

'I still don't understand where Romana and Vivien are,' ventured Emilia hesitantly.

'Well, neither do I,' came the Doctor's cheery confession. 'Not really. Ever heard of hyperspace?'

The Professor shook her head. 'No. What is it?'

K-9, now almost completely operational again, had listened to the conversation and decided to intervene on this question of fact. 'Hyperspace,' he said, 'is an exception of the special Theory of Relativity propounded by Einstein. Einstein's theory states—'

'Not now, K-9,' decreed the Doctor. 'Don't strain your database. You're not fully recovered yet.'

'Circuitry regeneration seventy-five per cent completed,' the automaton protested. Thanks to an enormous helping hand from the TARDIS, he was now able to complete the renewal process himself.

The Doctor spoke to him like an errant child. 'All the same, didn't I give you some calculations to do?'

'Calculations cannot be completed until you have finished the construction of the hyperspace drive, master,' concluded K-9.

'All right, all right,' replied the Doctor testily. 'Why don't you stop interrupting and let me get on with it, then?' He turned to the Professor to complain: 'He's a terrible gasbag, you know.'

But she was still trying to grasp some basic principles. 'I don't really understand about hyperspace,' she complained.

'Who does?' remarked the Doctor with a shrug. 'It's a pretty vague theory.'

'I understand it,' interjected K-9.

'Oh, shut up, K-9,' said the Doctor, not wishing to waste any more time. 'It's all to do with interspatial geometry, if you must know, Emilia.'

'What's that?' she asked. 'I've never heard of it. And I've certainly never studied it.'

'Nobody does any more,' he replied. 'They gave up teaching it two thousand years ago, even on Gallifrey. Altogether too hypothetical.'

'But hyperspace exists?'

'Oh, yes,' he agreed. 'Although most experts believe you're well advised to keep out of it. It's rather like finding the precise value of pi: you can get mixed up in calculations that never end. You can also get lost in there if you're not careful, like the Flying Dutchman. The problem is getting yourself out of hyperspace once you're in there. Not as easy as it sounds.'

'Is all this to do with the Time Distortion Effect?' asked the Professor, demonstrating a surprising knowledge of Einstein's Special Theory. 'You know, where he says that you cannot travel in space faster than the speed of light, because you'd arrive at your destination before you started out?'

'Something like that,' agreed the Doctor, secretly impressed. 'Of course, I do it all the time, but that's neither here nor there.'

'Oh.'

'No. Of course, there are other solutions to the problem – like space-warping and—'

'Hyperspace,' suggested the Professor, completing his sentence. 'And that's where Romana and Vivien are?'

'Actually they're still in the circle. Or whatever occupies that space in another dimension.'

All this talk of far-flung matters emboldened the

Professor to ask a question she had been longing to pose to her unpredictable companion. 'Doctor . . . are you from outer space?' she asked gently. 'If it's not too personal a question.'

'No, no,' he replied. 'Not outer space. I'm more from what you might call Inner Time.'

While the Professor digested that idea, the Doctor completed work on the piece of equipment he had brought with him. Privately, she thought the strange device looked like a patent hair dryer for French poodles, but she supposed he knew his own business best.

'Well, what do you think?' he asked K-9. 'Will it work?'

K-9 studied the problem carefully for a moment, then gave his verdict: 'Only on a setting of point-zero-zero-three-seven on the hyperspace scale, master.'

This came as an unwelcome shock to the Doctor, who had been hoping for a much better performance from his brainchild. 'If that's correct,' he complained, 'it means the circuits will burn out in about ten seconds flat.'

K-9 automatically corrected his master's maths. 'In 30.27 seconds precisely,' he said.

As far as the Doctor was concerned, that was only marginally better than his initial guess. It begged the question of whether a little over half a minute was time enough for him to enter hyperspace and then to leave it, with Romana in tow.

K-9's further conclusions did not reassure either. They were that the success of the mission would depend on where the Doctor landed: ideally that would be in, on or even under, something solid and secure. If, however, the initial point of impact was on something liquid or gaseous or, worst of all, moving, then all bets were off. You entered hyperspace, as the Professor put it, like Alice, through the rabbit hole. You left it the same way, through the same hole. Nothing must impede your departure or you might never get out at all.

'It's all very hit and miss,' admitted the Doctor. 'Fortunately, I'll be taking a piece of a chalk with me.'

'Why chalk?' asked the Professor.

'So I can mark precisely where the "rabbit hole" is on the other side of hyperspace. Then if I have to beat a hasty retreat, I can easily find the exit – by looking for the chalk mark.'

The old woman chuckled. 'Theseus used the same trick with the Minotaur in the Labyrinth.'

The Doctor looked vacant for a moment, as if lost in a memory. 'Yes, yes he did, didn't he,' he seemed to recall. 'Good old Theseus. Of course, he had a little help . . .'

It was pitch dark as K-9, the Doctor and the Professor emerged from the cottage. The weather had taken a turn for the worse, with a cold wind and driving rain. Holding the Professor's umbrella over the Doctor's machine, they staggered across the moor in the direction of the circle, which they reached without incident but soaking wet. Fortunately, K-9 had only recently been weatherproofed.

'Where do you want to put this beam thing?' asked the Professor.

'We'll leave that to K-9,' replied the Doctor. He then ordered the robot, 'Find the precise spot where Miss Fay was standing when she disappeared into hyperspace.'

'Affirmative, master,' replied the robot, heading for the place where Miss Fay had used her staff to burn a ring in the turf.

'Here,' he announced proudly.

The Doctor and the Professor placed the hyperspace drive about two metres from the spot. 'That should do it,' he said, adjusting the wire cone on the machine so that it pointed directly towards Miss Fay's take-off point.

'Do you understand what you've got to do?' he asked the Professor.

'I think so,' she replied. He had instructed her in her duties as they crossed the moor. Now that they had put the machine down, she went through the directions again. 'I push this switch down, on your signal,' she said, indicating a button at the side of the machine. 'Then I watch the dial, and when the needle on the dial registers point zero zero three seven, I pull down this lever.'

'Right,' confirmed the Doctor. 'But remember,

you've only got thirty seconds before you must switch off again. If you wait too long – pow!'

'Pow?' queried the Professor.

'A technical expression meaning that all this beautiful micro-circuitry will fuse into a puddle of molten metal about the size of my fist.'

'I see,' said the Professor. 'But what happens if the Ogri come back while you're wherever you'll be?'

'That's where K-9 comes in. He'll generate a force field a touch more sophisticated than Miss Fay's, and that should keep them out for a while.'

'For how long?'

K-9 raised his head. 'My power packs will be drained in approximately seventeen minutes, thirty-one point eight-six seconds.'

'There you are,' said the Doctor. 'Now, if the Ogri break through, run as if something very nasty were after you, because something very nasty will be after you.'

'But what about you? How will you get back?'

'Simple. Just switch on the ray for thirty seconds, say, every half-hour.'

The Professor shrugged. 'Very well. If you think that'll work . . .'

'Well, of course it'll work!' The Doctor smiled genially at her. 'Shall we give it a try?'

K-9 cleared the area, and together they went through the technical procedure without a hitch. The numbers on the dial rose until it registered .0037 and then, at the

Doctor's signal, the Professor pulled down the lever. There was a flash of light, some black smoke, and an unpleasant smell of burnt vinegar. But nothing happened. The Doctor remained on the piece of charred turf. He did not vanish into hyperspace.

'Switch off, Emilia, would you?' he said calmly. It was frustrating, but experience told him that things didn't always go right first time.

As instructed, the Professor switched everything off. She turned to the Doctor and asked anxiously, 'Was it me? Did I do something wrong?'

But K-9 quickly moved to console her. 'There is an error in the circuitry of the machine. You are not to blame.'

Irritated, the Doctor attacked the circuit pack on the machine with his screwdriver. 'I can't think what went wrong,' he complained.

'I can,' announced the mobile computer. 'A faulty connection in the circuitry. Here.' K-9 indicated the place with a beam of light from his nose laser.

Grumbling to himself, the Doctor made a few adjustments, replaced the casing and turned to the others, declaring, 'There you are – good as new. Let's try again.'

Suddenly K-9's warning light began to flash. 'Danger. Ogri approaching from the south-west.'

The Professor peered into the darkness but couldn't see anything.

'Are you ready?' asked the Doctor, a new note of urgency in his voice.

'Just a minute,' trembled the Professor.

K-9 repeated his warning. 'Ogri approaching! Ogri approaching! Fifty metres and closing!'

'Same procedure as before, Emilia. Ready?' the Doctor asked again.

'Ready,' confirmed the Professor, who was desperately trying to remember what she had done the last time. Come on – concentrate, old girl, she told herself. First switch – then lever.

'Ogri, forty metres and closing,' proclaimed K-9.

The Professor waited for the dial to register. At last she announced, 'Point nought nought three seven ... Holding.'

'Ogri – twenty-eight metres and closing.'

'Now!' shouted the Doctor, and the Professor threw the lever. There was a blinding flash of light, another strong smell of burning ...

This time, the Doctor vanished into thin air.

At the same time, K-9 turned and fixed his laser beam on the Ogri at almost point-blank range.

'Romana,' called the Doctor. 'Romana!'

His voice echoed in what was apparently the interior of some large ship. He had materialised at an intersection of blank, white-walled corridors. With only a short time available in which to find Romana, he headed into one at random, soon finding it lined with equally faceless cabin doors.

The Doctor wondered what kind of vessel this was. A passenger ship, perhaps? In which case, where were the passengers and crew, and why was everything so plain and functional? Clearly this was no luxury liner. The cabins were locked on the outside, as if to prevent their occupants from getting out. With the aid of his sonic screwdriver, he began cautiously to unlock the cabin doors, one by one.

Inside many of them he was startled to find the skeletal remains of creatures from all corners of the galaxy, some of which even he couldn't identify. They seemed to have come from numerous different planets, and each was shackled to the wall of its cell. Had he stumbled on a zoo in hyperspace? But that was absurd.

Then it came to him. Of course – cells! This was a prison ship! A secure container in which dangerous criminals were housed away from their home planets. A kind of Devil's Island in hyperspace. Somehow the ship must have run aground, leaving crew, guards and inmates stranded. From what the Doctor could tell of the wizened corpses, everyone had died at about the same time, suggesting that some awful calamity had befallen the whole ship. He redoubled his search, calling out his companion's name repeatedly.

Romana, meanwhile, had just regained consciousness to find herself in a cell, chained to a long dead octopoidal creature that must have weighed half a tonne when alive. Now it was just a pile of wrinkled skin, from which protruded something that looked like horns. She shuddered. A horned octopus: a creature from nightmares if ever there was one. In order to make sure the thing was dead, she leaned over and kicked its remains. A cloud of dust rose, but nothing more, and she breathed a sigh of relief.

It was then that she heard the Doctor calling. She cried out hoarsely in reply, coughing as she ingested a mouthful of horned-octopus dust. A moment later, the door to her cell opened.

'All change at Venus for the Brighton line,' the Doctor called in cheerfully.

Romana was not amused. 'Where have you been?' she asked grumpily. 'What's happening? Where am I?'

'Well, in strict order of asking,' said the Doctor, 'busy – nothing – hyperspace.' He examined the pile of wrinkled skin beside her and tutted sympathetically. 'Your friend doesn't look too well.'

'This can't be hyperspace,' she said.

'Why not?' he said, using the sonic screwdriver to release her from the chains.

She rubbed her wrists gratefully. 'It can't be hyperspace because everyone knows hyperspace is a theoretical absurdity.'

'All except the people who built the ship four thousand years ago,' the Doctor pointed out. 'This is a hyperspace vessel if I ever saw one. I admit it isn't the smartest piece of space engineering I've ever seen, but for a prison ship it isn't too bad. In the nineteenth century, the British used to put convicted criminals into hulks like this moored in the River Thames, until they could decide what to do with them. Well, it was either that or Australia.' It was obvious from Romana's expression that she was in no mood for a lecture on Earth penal history. So he suggested, 'Let's go and explore.'

Typical, she thought. Not, let's find out what Miss Fay is up to and put a stop to it – but let's explore. If anything defined the Doctor it was that: curiosity. What was round the next corner, over the next hill, on the next planet. She gave a wry smile. 'Let's find the control room.'

They set off in search of the flight deck and came across several official-looking signs on the walls, mostly written in scripts neither of them could read. That in itself was unusual.

'What do you suppose that means?' asked Romana, pointing to a particularly elaborate sign. It seemed to consist mainly of dots and stars.

'Probably something boring like "No ball games in the corridor",' he ventured. The corridor they were walking down widened until it debouched into a large space the size of a parade ground. At one end, the spiral ramps rose to a higher level, which was protected by thick glass.

'I bet that's where the crew can be found,' observed the Doctor.

They mounted the ramp and found the door to the flight deck open. But there was no flight crew present and no desiccated remains either. Just a series of empty seats in front of various video display units. The whole place was clean and dust free.

'It looks as if Vivien Fay has been busy tidying up,' said the Doctor.

'Then why is the ship still here?' asked Romana.

'I suspect you can't fly this thing solo, as a precaution to prevent it from being hijacked. You probably need a whole crew. I mean, just look at that flight console – it's immensely complex. There's no way one person could control all that – not even the resourceful Miss Fay. She doesn't strike me as an experienced hyperspace engineer.'

'Then what's she doing here?' demanded Romana. 'If she *is* here, that is.'

The Doctor pondered, then said, 'Try this for size. Suppose she was one of the convicts being held here. Somehow she got free and managed to kill everyone on board – only then she found she couldn't fly the ship on her own. So now she's stuck here with the Ogri, who only do her bidding as long as she keeps feeding them blood.'

'That can't be easy. I wonder what would happen if she stopped feeding them?'

'They'd kill her. Presumably her veins are full of the stuff they need. I shouldn't think the Ogri are big on loyalty or friendship. Remember, they're cannibals on their own planet. To them anything that moves is simply lunch on the hoof. So, keep an eye out for them.'

Romana shuddered and almost felt pity for Miss Fay. Fancy being cooped up here all that time with only Ogri for company, she thought. I bet they're not big on conversation.

'Is much known about the Ogri?' she asked.

'Not a lot.' The Doctor was fiddling with the controls of a monitor screen. 'One experience of Ogros, and most visitors – of which there haven't been many in the last few thousand years – go somewhere else for their holidays.'

An image had come up on the screen. 'Look at that,' he said. 'Just as I thought.' It showed the circle of stones, and above it was the outline of a large spaceship.

'According to that display,' deduced Romana, 'we can only be a few metres above the stones. Why couldn't we see the ship from down there?'

'Because the ship is in a different kind of space from the circle.'

'In other words, hyperspace. Rather than the ordinary, four-dimensional space we operate in.'

'By Jove, she's got it,' he chortled, meanwhile activating other screens, which began issuing forth a steady stream of data. 'This thing didn't run out of fuel,' he announced. 'There's enough power to take her almost anywhere in the galaxy. And, as far as I can tell, the drive unit is still operational. Romana, this ship didn't run aground. It came to a stop because there was no one on the bridge still able to navigate it. They were all dead or dying. And that left Vivien Fay and a few Ogri in charge of a complex piece of machinery they didn't know how to operate. With no trained hyperspace engineers on ancient Earth, there wasn't anybody she could turn to to help her out. So she's just been patiently pottering about in southern England for the four thousand years since. She must have worked out how to put the ship in stasis, preserved in aspic until she needed it. But why now?'

Romana had an uneasy answer to that. 'Possibly because we're on the scene?'

The Doctor was disconcerted. 'I don't think being Vivien Fay's pet hyperspace engineer can be regarded as secure, long-term employment, Romana. Once she's learnt how to run the ship you're finger-food for the Ogri.'

She nodded. 'Speaking of which, where are they, do you think?'

'Somewhere nearby,' he guessed. 'Let's take a look around.'

They began investigating cabins on the upper deck. Here they found several humanoid skeletons, clearly the remains of members of the crew, who had been off-duty when the catastrophe – whatever it was – had struck. They also found a couple of dormitories, which seemed to have been accommodation for prison guards.

'If the ship's just come out of stasis,' said the Doctor, 'all this organic matter could rapidly decompose. Have you still got the Tracer with you?' he asked.

Romana produced it from her belt, switched it on, and was rewarded with a feeble bleeping. 'That settles it. The segment must be somewhere aboard this ship.'

Inside the stone circle, K-9 and the Professor were finding things difficult. There were now two Ogri, and they kept trying to break through K-9's force field. Each attack bit deeper into the automaton's power reserves. The Professor did her best not to become distracted. According to her watch, it was nearly time to switch on the Doctor's hyperspace transmitter, so that he and Romana could return from their theoretical absurdity.

'Power depleted,' announced K-9. 'I cannot hold the Ogri for much longer.'

That sounded like defeatist talk to the Professor. It was time to rally her troops. 'Come on, K-9,' she said encouragingly. 'Where's that Dunkirk spirit? Never say die, you know.'

'I never do,' he replied. 'Yet my power packs will only last for a limited length of time. When they are exhausted, the Ogri will destroy us.'

'Just hold it a fraction longer, can you? It's time for me to switch on the transmitter.'

'Quickly,' the robot dog gasped.

The Professor threw the lever, and a vortex of light emerged from the charred turf where the Doctor had disappeared. But no figures appeared in it.

'I hope nothing's happened to them,' she sighed, wondering what on earth she would do if they didn't return. She couldn't see herself calling on Constable Trescothick of Bodcombe Parva and explaining what had happened to two complete strangers who had appeared out of nowhere. Her previous experience of the local law had been unhappy – a matter of riding her bicycle without lights. And, of course, she was well known to the Chief Constable because of her campaign to prevent the Secretary of St Olaf's Golf Club from removing a dolmen from the fairway. 'He thinks I'm a nutcase already,' she told herself. 'After this he'll want to have me sectioned.'

It suddenly dawned on her that things had gone very quiet. No complaints from K-9 – and no sound of the Ogri trying to break through the force field.

'Are you all right, K-9?' she asked.

But the robot did not reply. She looked around and saw the two Ogri standing still. Then, as if at a word of command, they turned and moved off into the night.

'Did you see that, K-9? The Ogri are going. They're giving up.'

K-9 replied slowly, as if every word was costing him a huge effort – which it was. 'Assumption . . . incorrect,' he gasped. 'They are going. But not giving up.'

The Professor knelt beside the little fellow. His glowing amber eye screen was now very faint. 'How are you, my dear?'

'Power exhausted,' K-9 replied.

The Doctor had mentioned that this might happen. 'Can you recharge yourself?'

'Given time.'

The Professor had another very pertinent question. 'Where do you think the Ogri are off to?'

K-9 stuttered, 'Suggest they have gone to recharge, too.'

It seemed an obvious enough reply. But the question remained: 'How?' The Ogri weren't robots: they couldn't just recharge themselves, could they?

'They will need to ingest more globulin,' explained K-9.

'But that means finding more blood.'

'Affirmative.'

Professor Rumford shrank into her duffel coat and looked sightlessly into the dark night. 'That means they're going to kill somebody, doesn't it?'

K-9 did not reply.

Pat Blount and Zac Hardcastle had been an item ever since their first day in Miss Gilbey's class at Reservoir

Road Primary. Pat had disliked Zac on sight, whereupon she had hit him with her lunchbox and made him cry. One of her mum's horrible egg sandwiches apparently made him feel better, and thereafter for the next few years they swapped sandwiches – until senior school when the local chippy took care of their various dietary needs. They went to uni together and shared digs, which should have put an end to any future liaison, but in fact it didn't. They applied for jobs at the same firm – an insurance company on the outskirts of a once prosperous Lancashire mill town. They also bought a small, rather scruffy flat, which they shared with a marmalade cat called Ivan and a budgie called Walter.

Aware that their lifestyle lacked a certain pizazz, they made up for it by acquiring an elderly car and a smart, nearly new tent, and took holidays abroad, leaving Ivan and Walter in the care of their parents. But this year they had decided to give unspoilt Britain a chance. They had driven south, stopping at various places, all of which had been insufficiently unspoilt to tempt them to stay. Then they had arrived at Bodcombe Parva, which looked promising.

So they had gone to the Wheatsheaf for a drink and directions. Did anyone know of a place where they could pitch their tent – somewhere wild and away from civilisation? No one ever went near the Nine Travellers, they were told. The area was said to be haunted; it was certainly a scary place at night. But Pat and Zac had braved continental campsites from Denmark to the Pyrenees, and felt more than capable of coping with a West Country stone circle. So, they had parked their car, collected their gear, and tramped across the moor.

About three-quarters of a mile from the circle, they found a convenient hollow where they could pitch their tent out of the prevailing wind. They lit the Primus stove, had supper, and settled down in their sleeping bags for the night.

At around 3am, Pat woke with a start. 'What's that?' she whispered. She had heard a movement outside their tent.

'What?' asked Zac, having been wrenched from a dream about fishing.

The noise came again – a sort of shuffling.

'That,' she said. 'There's something out there. What is it?'

'Dunno,' Zac replied blearily, showing little inclination to find out. In similar circumstances last year, in Brittany, he had encountered two inquisitive llamas in the early hours of the morning. The experience had left him disinclined to investigate strange noises in the middle of the night.

But Pat was gently shaking him awake. 'Take the torch and go and see. It may be someone lost on the moor.'

That didn't seem at all likely, but he knew she just wanted to have her mind put at rest. 'If it is, how are we going to be able to help?' he asked. 'We're strangers here ourselves.'

'You're always putting things off,' she complained. 'Like that time when you were going to have the brakes fixed on the car. Remember?'

He remembered only too well – it was how he had lost his no claims bonus. In his view, the past was another country best left undisturbed, but women seemed to revel in its potential for conflict between the sexes. So, grumbling, and with Pat pushing him out of the nice warm sleeping bag, he found the torch and crawled outside.

'Good grief!' she heard him say when he got outside. 'Pat, you've got to come out here. You'll never believe this.'

So she joined him in the chilly, damp air. Facing them were two huge stones, roughly oblong in shape, like something out of Stonehenge. 'Where have they come from?' she gasped.

'How should I know?' said Zac. 'They weren't there when we went to bed. Otherwise we'd have seen them.'

'It's probably a joke,' she decided. 'You know, let's scare these northern yobs.' She put on her scary local voice: '"Nobody goes near the Nine Travellers at Night." I bet someone from the Wheatsheaf dumped them here after closing time.'

'But they must weigh tonnes,' Zac pointed out. 'Besides, why would they do that? Doesn't make sense to scare away the people with money to spend.'

Pat went over and stood next to one. 'They're probably plastic. I bet we could push them over if we tried.' She put her hands on the nearest stone and pushed.

Something gleamed in the depths of the rock, and suddenly Pat found herself arm-deep inside. She screamed hysterically but couldn't pull loose. Her flesh was glowing, bubbling against the stone.

Horrified, Zac went to help her, but the other Ogri moved too fast. He found himself rooted to the spot with the stone creature at his back, sucking him into its interior. A hideous sound, half heartbeat, half roar, filled the night air as Zac's own agonised shouts for help ebbed away along with the rest of him.

After both Pat and Zac had disappeared, the Ogri remained static for a few minutes while digestion took place. Then, following a quiet eructation, the remains of the campers, including bones and shoes and anything else the Ogri deemed inedible, were extruded like pellets from an owl.

Interlude

A Short Guide to Justice Machines

The possibility of creating a single universal code of law for every planet has long been a dream of intergalactic lawmakers everywhere. And almost everywhere it has been rejected on the grounds that the very multiplicity of species represents a problem that defies rational solution. How do you include in any legal format some of the more bizarre life forms to be found in the universe, such as the cloud creatures of Neri or the giant amoebas of Amphitrite, whose very identity keeps changing with the constant division of cells?

In order to simplify the legal process and bring clarity to certain obscure areas of the law, some planets have opted for Justice Machines. Judge and jury, prosecution and defence (and – if required – executioner), all rolled into one, these machines are seen to have certain advantages over statutory law. They are infallible, inflexible, and allow no grey areas of judgement. A law has either been broken or it has not. If it has, then the lawbreaker will be punished. If it hasn't, the defendant will go free. Complex legal arguments do not sway machines: therefore, lawyers become irrelevant and, as a result, few in number. Hence trials are shorter. Mechanical proceedings can go from accusation to sentence – even execution – in as little as twenty minutes, in which time machines have analysed all aspects of the case, heard all legal arguments, arrived at a conclusion and carried out the sentence of the court. Another advantage of Justice Machines is that they eliminate the possibility of anyone exerting undue influence on judge or jury. You cannot bribe or intimidate a machine.

At least, that is the theory.

Chapter VIII

The Megara

The Doctor and Romana were still examining the cabins on the flight deck. He rubbed one of the compartment windows and peered inside.

'Anything?' she asked.

'I don't think so. Certainly nothing alive. Or, indeed, anything I'd like to meet if it *was* alive. Mind you,' he observed, continuing along the corridor, 'I'll tell you one thing – if anyone has survived, it's going to be apocalyptically furious about the hold-up ... I mean, how do you apologise for leaving someone for four thousand years in hyperspace? You can hardly blame the weather, can you? Or leaves on the line.'

Romana had noticed something. 'Wait a moment. This compartment's a different colour from the rest.' She pointed to a red door to which were attached several large plastic seals. 'What do they say?'

The Doctor examined the seals, but once again found them indecipherable. 'I can't read the script without the TARDIS here to translate,' he confessed. 'It probably says, "Do not open. Penalty Fifty Pounds."' He stood on tiptoe and tried to peer in through the window. 'Can't see a thing.'

'Perhaps we might be best to leave it,' suggested Romana.

'Nonsense,' he replied. 'I don't like closed doors. Keeps the world out.'

So he broke the seals and opened the door. 'Not a thing,' he said.

Then suddenly two shining silver globes emerged, floating in mid-air.

'Hello! Life at last.' He put out a hand to touch one of the globes, and withdrew it rapidly when the contact burned.

The globe spoke: 'It is not permitted to touch the Megara.' The voice was thin and reedy, and decidedly artificial.

The Doctor licked his hand and apologised immediately. 'I beg your pardon,' he said. 'But I don't understand. Who or what are the Megara?'

'We are,' it announced. 'We are the Megara. We are Justice Machines.'

'We are the Law,' declared the second globe in a similar vocal tone.

'Judge, jury and executioner.'

'Once we have arrived at our verdict – which usually does not take long . . .'

'. . . we execute it,' said the First Megara.

'Without fear or favour.'

'Utterly impartially,' remarked the First Megara with grim satisfaction. They were like Tweedledum and Tweedledee.

The Doctor chose to be diplomatic. His experience of Justice Machines was limited, but by and large it had not been happy. Machine Law was, in his view, all right for machines, but it usually proved too inflexible when dealing with the behaviour of the biologically diverse.

'It's a great relief,' he said, 'to know that the law is in such capable – er – hands. Pity we must be going now.' He began moving away as quickly as he could. 'Goodbye,' he said brightly to the silver globes.

Romana was intrigued by the Megara and anticipated no threat from them. She couldn't understand the Doctor's obvious apprehension. 'What's the matter?' she hissed.

'Come on,' he muttered. 'Just keep moving.'

But the Megara had other ideas. They were not going to allow two strangers who had been found wandering around their ship to escape so easily.

'Stay!' they ordered, and to make it clear that they were serious one of them fired an electronic warning beam at the Doctor and Romana. It did them no serious damage but did sting sufficiently to make them wince.

'Do not move,' commanded the First Megara.

'Which of you,' demanded the Second, 'removed the great seals?'

The Doctor put his hand up, like a naughty boy in class. 'I did,' he said. 'I cannot tell a lie. I removed the seals because I feared for your Honours' safety.'

The Megara consulted: the two globes were almost touching.

'He meant well,' observed the First Megara.

'But the Law clearly states that no one may remove the seals without authorisation,' came the reply. 'The penalty is death.'

The First Megara turned to the Doctor and asked: 'Where is your authorisation? We must verify it.'

The Doctor went into his best apologetic mode: dignified but respectful. 'I'm sorry,' he said. 'I didn't know I needed authorisation. You see, I'm a stranger here myself, your Honours. But I can promise you I won't remove any seals ever again without the proper authorisation in writing!'

The First Megara seemed to be impressed by the Doctor's eloquence. 'Contrition,' it observed to its fellow jurist, 'is to be accounted in the accused's favour.'

'Ignorance of the Law is not,' declared the second silver globe.

Sparks flashed between the two, followed by a metallic buzzing, as if each globe was a hive of bees.

'I will undertake his defence,' announced the First Megara.

'Very well,' replied the Second. 'However, I think you should advise your client that there is little likelihood of clemency.'

'I will so advise him,' agreed Megara One, then, realising that the Doctor and Romana had taken advantage of the impromptu legal conference to escape, it added, 'He has gone!'

'There you are,' said the Second Megara. 'Further proof of his guilt.'

'Ill-judged, I agree,' said the First Megara. 'But of little import. None can escape the Megara, no matter how far or fast they may travel.'

The buzzing between the two globes immediately ceased: clearly some kind of agreement had been reached. They followed the Doctor and Romana down the corridor, moving in a leisurely manner as if confident that their quarry could not escape.

The Professor and K-9 had taken up their positions in the circle again. The dog-shaped computer was standing guard beside the machine the Doctor had built, whilst Emilia was pacing up and down looking for the return of the Ogri. Finally, she announced, 'I can't see those creatures anywhere. Are you fully recharged yet?'

'Negative,' replied K-9. 'Recharging incomplete. Nevertheless, it is time to switch on the beam again.'

The Professor checked her watch and agreed: 'You're right, it's been thirty minutes. Just a couple of seconds to go.' She prepared the hyperspace drive for the switchover. 'At least we haven't got those creatures breathing down our necks this time.'

'Now!' said K-9.

The Professor pressed down the lever, and a vortex of light appeared in the area of burned turf. This time a figure did appear inside the circle, but it was neither the Doctor nor Romana.

Instead, it was Miss Fay, staff in hand. She stepped menacingly forward.

The Professor reacted with indignation. How dare Vivien appear in her circle, summoned by her machine!

K-9 was equally protective. 'Do not touch that machine, Miss Fay,' he warned. 'Or else I will be forced to stun you.'

Miss Fay appeared more amused than frightened by the threat. 'My dear little robot,' she said, 'you haven't enough power left to strike a match – let alone inconvenience me.'

As if to prove her point, K-9 advanced a few inches, then came spluttering to an ignominious halt.

'See what I mean,' said Vivien Fay. 'Powerless.'

The Professor attempted to appeal to her friend: 'Vivien. If you'd only listen to reason . . .'

'Reason!' screamed the Cailleach, for that was who she was. 'I've had enough of reason. All I want is to escape. I've been stuck here for thousands of years, with no end in sight. Can you imagine what it's been like? A living nightmare. Every time I've tried to escape something went wrong. First, the ship, then the local tribes turning on me. Now you. Don't make me kill you, Emilia.' She pointed her staff at the Doctor's machine.

'No!' The Professor reacted with horror. 'They can't get back if you—'

'Good,' declared Miss Fay. 'Then they'll find out what it's been like for me all these years.'

She made a simple gesture with her staff, and the machine was irradiated with a blue light. In a matter of seconds, it had become a molten heap of metal.

'There you are,' she said. 'With my compliments.' She moved towards the edge of the circle, pausing to call out: 'Ogri! Come! I command you!'

Out of the darkness came the two stone creatures, to stand beside the Professor and K-9 and await further orders.

The Doctor and Romana were still running down the ship's corridors, pursued by the Megara.

'I marked the point where I entered hyperspace,' panted the Doctor. 'Should be somewhere around here. Look for a chalk mark. X marks the spot.'

Romana looked back and saw the two globes approaching. 'The sooner the better,' she puffed. 'They're still following us.'

'What do you expect? They're Justice Machines. Not flesh and blood and sore feet. They don't know the meaning of "Let's stop for a bit while we catch our breath". They'll keep going for ever if they have to.' He paused for a moment to look round for his chalk mark. 'The projector the Professor is using has a small spread. So, we've got to be in exactly the right place for when she switches on. Which –' he said, checking his watch – 'should be any time now. I hope.'

Romana stopped running and pointed to the deck. 'There,' she said. 'There's your mark.'

'Quick,' gasped the Doctor. 'Come on.'

They stood precisely in the centre of the large X chalked on the floor, and waited and waited . . .

'Nothing,' said Romana.

But a little way away from them, along the corridor, a vortex of light appeared. Thinking that the Professor had somehow moved the position of the machine in the circle, Romana and the Doctor ran towards it. But as they approached, three figures materialised in front of them – Miss Fay and her two Ogri. The Cailleach's mocking laughter echoed around the empty spaceship.

'Too late, Doctor,' she said. 'Too late!'

Chapter IX

The Secret of Vivien Fay

'There's no way out for you,' declared Miss Fay with an air of great satisfaction. 'You're both trapped here like flies in amber. Enjoy hyperspace, my friends. You have all the time in existence.'

Impulsively the Doctor attempted to seize her, but the Ogri anticipated his move and came to stand either side of her, providing a guard he could not overpower.

'Don't worry,' she said, 'I'll come to visit you from time to time. Every few years or so.'

It was at this point that the Megara appeared in the corridor. 'Do not harm our prisoner,' they warned. 'Step away from him. All communication is forbidden.'

Miss Fay had never met the two jurists before, and even after all this time had been only partially able to decipher bits of the writing on the Great Seals. This was explicit enough: 'IT IS ABSOLUTELY FORBIDDEN TO BREAK ANY OF THESE SEALS ON PAIN OF INSTANT DEATH.' The rest was in incomprehensible Tau Cetian legalese, thus preventing any but the most obdurate Tau Cetian lawyer from making any sense of it.

Miss Fay, who was not a Tau Cetian lawyer, had presumed that the injunction referred to some physical danger, like a fuel store or some dangerous equipment, and had sensibly left well enough alone.

'Did you break the seals?' she asked the Doctor.

'Well, yes,' he replied. 'I'm very much afraid I did.'

'Not a clever move,' she suggested.

'Silence!' snapped the First Megara. 'The prisoner is ours and is incommunicado.'

'Afterwards,' suggested the Second Megara, 'we may perhaps allow you to have him. His corpse at any rate, if you have a use for such things.'

'Oh, I do,' she agreed. 'I do. How soon may I have it?'

The Doctor appealed to the Megara. 'Please don't rush on my account. Take your time. Consider your verdict.'

'We already have,' replied the Second Megara. 'We have found you guilty and passed sentence. This will now be carried out by myself as Prosecutor.'

'What sentence?' asked the Doctor. 'I wasn't aware of a trial. Not to mention anything like a verdict.'

'The verdict,' explained the First Megara calmly, 'was guilty as charged. The sentence was death. With the execution to be carried out immediately.'

'May I watch?' asked Miss Fay. She turned to the Doctor. 'You don't mind, do you?'

'Be my guest,' replied the Doctor. 'Come one, come all.'

The Second Megara hovered about a foot from the Doctor's head. 'Prepare for dissolution,' it said.

'I object,' said the Doctor suddenly.

'On what grounds?' enquired Megara Two. 'Everything was done according to the Law. There are no grounds for any objections.'

'How can there be a sentence when there hasn't been a trial?'

'There has been a trial,' insisted the silver globe.

'But I wasn't there,' objected the Doctor. 'It was in my absence.'

'That is because your presence was not required,' the First Megara explained, with what could almost pass as an electronic sigh. 'I would refer you,' it went on, 'to the Legal Code Rules of the Law, Volume 2. Subsection: Trials. Paragraph 215. There it states quite clearly that in the event of insanity, flight, unconsciousness or any of a dozen or more different eventualities – which at this stage I will not elucidate, unless you insist . . .'

The Doctor shook his head. The trouble with machines, he thought, was they had no sense of humour, no sense of proportionality. They always went on to the bitter end.

'. . . the presence of the defendant is not a prerequisite of any such legal proceedings.'

'I should still have been there,' he pronounced.

'But why?' asked the apparently mystified machine.

'So that I could have spoken in my own defence.'

'I defended you,' said Megara One.

'I was judge,' said Megara Two. 'And believe me, your counsel was most eloquent on your behalf. I have rarely heard a more succinct speech in mitigation . . .'

'Nevertheless, I should have been there to make it,' insisted the Doctor. 'I demand a retrial and the right to defend myself.'

Lights flashed from the Megara, and their buzzing rose to a crescendo. 'It is not permitted,' they eventually said in unison.

'Why not?' enquired the Doctor.

'Because you are a humanoid biological life form and therefore incapable of understanding the subtleties of the Law.'

'Machine Law,' said the Doctor in disgust.

'Of course,' they replied drily. 'There is none other worthy of the name.'

Megara One, in its role as counsel for the defence, offered its client some advice. 'I suggest,' it said, 'you submit to execution willingly. It is so much easier for everyone in the end.'

'I intend to appeal against my sentence,' declared the Doctor. He had been in enough courtrooms across the universe to know how these things worked.

'But there are no legal grounds for such a course of action,' protested Megara One. 'None at all.'

The Doctor raised an eyebrow. 'How do you know? You haven't heard my case yet.'

'It would be a waste of time to do so. It would also be cruel to raise your hopes.'

'Let me be the judge of that,' said the Doctor. 'I'm the one about to be executed. Remember?'

While the globes conferred together once more, amid flashes of blue light and much mechanical buzzing, Miss Fay decided to step in and speed up the proceedings.

'Your Honours,' she said smoothly, her voice the essence of sweetness and light, 'surely you are not going to allow yourselves to be persuaded by this criminal. It is clearly just a ruse on his part.'

Megara Two turned angrily on Miss Fay. 'Who are you?' it demanded. 'Identify yourself to the Court.'

'I am Vivien Fay, your Honours, of Rose Cottage, Bodcombe.'

The name clearly meant nothing to the Megara. 'Explain yourself. As briefly and logically as you are able.'

Romana, who had been waiting patiently all this time, could contain herself no longer. 'You can't believe her,' she insisted. 'She's the reason why we're here.'

'Are you suggesting that this Vivien Fay broke the seals?' asked Megara Two.

'No,' admitted Romana, 'but—'

'Then your evidence is immaterial and incompetent. I would warn you that attempts to influence the Bench are punishable by death. And will not be tolerated. In accordance with Article 14 of the Code, subsection 135,' it continued, 'this humanoid's execution is stayed for two hours while we graciously consent to hear his appeal. Afterwards, executions will take place as ordered.'

The Doctor bowed. 'Your Honours are too kind,' he said.

But this was not soon enough for Miss Fay. 'I demand that you execute him!' she insisted. 'If you don't, he'll escape.'

'Demand!' The very word seemed to render Megara Two apoplectic. 'You have no right to demand anything of the Megara. We are not your servants. And as for escaping. Do you not know that none may escape the Megara?'

'Oh dear, Vivien, I think you've upset them,' observed the Doctor cheerfully.

Meanwhile, the Professor had managed to lift the Doctor's robot dog onto the altar stone, where it now sat as if awaiting sacrifice. In truth, she had thought the end had come for them both when the Ogri had come so horribly close. But Vivien had summoned them away with her in a storm of light, without a word.

How rude, the Professor thought to herself. Still. Better dismissed than dead.

With a screwdriver in one hand, she stood over K-9 like some vengeful priestess, wondering which part of his anatomy to attack first. Unfortunately, she couldn't find any access to the innards of the machine and knew that, even if she did, she wouldn't have the slightest idea of what to do.

'I feel so helpless,' she said. She absentmindedly touched the screwdriver to K-9's neck and was rewarded with movement, as he suddenly lifted his head.

'Oh, thank heavens,' she said. 'Are you all right?'

'Thank you, Professor,' replied K-9.

'Can you move?'

'Mobility impaired. But databanks recharged.'

The Professor decided that the robot dog was strong enough to face the bad news. 'Vivien smashed the crystal-ray gadget,' she said. 'The Doctor and Romana can't possibly return now. What are we going to do?'

K-9 had no doubts. 'Reconstruct the machine,' he said simply.

'How?'

'With your help,' explained K-9. 'It is not difficult. The Doctor could build it. So can we.'

The Professor disagreed. 'I dig things up,' she said. 'I don't build them. We need an engineer for that.'

'You can become an engineer,' replied K-9. 'Under my directions, of course.'

Yet the Professor wasn't so sure. If archaeology had taught her anything, it was to dismiss easy solutions to complex problems.

*

Romana and the Doctor were discussing courtroom tactics in the corridor of the hyperspace vessel. Now, she believed, was the time to play their trump card.

'Which is?' enquired the Doctor.

'Tell them who you are. Tell them you're a Time Lord,' she insisted.

He snorted. 'A Time Lord who can't get off their wretched prison ship. I don't think that's going to impress them.'

'Of course it will. They're sure to have heard of the Time Lords. They'll be in awe of us. They'll probably bow down and want to worship us.'

The Doctor laughed. 'In case you hadn't noticed, they're globes – they can't bow down! Besides, I'm sure there'll be something in that Code of Law of theirs which will forbid them from giving in to pressure from an uppity biological life form. They'll probably find an excuse to disintegrate us slowly, an inch at a time.'

Romana didn't normally have to cajole him into action, but she persevered. 'They're just machines. Someone like us made them. They must realise that we are superior to them.'

'I doubt it,' replied the Doctor. 'I heard of a galactic federation once. Lots of different life forms arguing amongst themselves. So they built a Justice Machine to administer the Law.'

She wondered where this was leading. 'What happened?'

'It found the federation in contempt of court and blew up the entire galaxy.'

'But that's ridiculous,' commented Romana.

The Doctor nodded, in a philosophical sort of way. 'That's what the federation's leaders all said, as minute particles of them were distributed amongst the stars.'

After a prolonged burst of buzzing and flashing, the Megara had reached a decision. Megara Two bustled up to the Doctor and said, 'The court has considered the request of the humanoid, hereinafter known as the Doctor. In order to speed up the process of law, it will graciously permit him to conduct his own appeal prior to his execution.'

'Thank you, your Honour,' deadpanned the Doctor.

'You may call your first witness.'

The Doctor bowed. 'I call as my first witness Miss Romanadvoratrelundar.'

Romana reacted in astonishment. She had not expected this.

'The witness will take the stand and be sworn in,' declared Megara Two.

Romana moved towards the holographic image of a small, raised platform with a rail around it, which had appeared as if from nowhere, apparently generated by the Megara. 'The witness,' continued the Megara, 'will repeat after me: I swear to tell the truth . . .'

'I swear to tell the truth . . .'

'. . . as far as I, a mere humanoid . . .'

'. . . as far as I—' Romana abruptly stopped. 'Look, I object to the wording,' she said.

'You cannot,' declared Megara Two. 'If you wish to give evidence, you must swear according to the Law. If you do not, either your evidence will be ignored or, should it not be ignored, you will be held in contempt of court for expressing your views in such a disrespectful manner. Punishment for that is death.'

The Doctor intervened smoothly. 'I'm sure my witness wishes to withdraw her last remarks. Don't you, Romana?' he said.

Megara Two addressed Romana directly: 'Do you?' it asked.

Romana swallowed hard and nodded. She remembered where she had got to in the oath, and repeated the offensive wording: '. . . as far as I, a mere humanoid . . .'

'. . . am capable of knowing the truth,' went on Megara Two. This in turn she duly repeated. At this point the First Megara extended a thin metallic arm which landed itself on Romana's head in a vice-like grip. When she tried to shake it free, nothing happened. The connection was too strong. In fact, filaments from the Megara had imperceptibly invaded her brain.

'What is this?' she demanded.

'It is a method for assessing the level of truth of any statements you make.'

'But I've already sworn to tell the truth!'

'The promises of biological life forms are unreliable

in our experience,' observed Megara Two. 'We find that direct contact with the cerebral cortex of the witness is much more precise than trusting to the vagaries of an individual whose concept of truth may be equivocal to say the least.'

Romana decided to cease struggling and accept the invasion. 'What happens if your machine detects that the level of truth has fallen during the interrogation?'

'Something most regrettable, Miss Romanadvoratrelundar,' remarked Megara Two. 'Tragic, one might even say.'

For a machine, it had a well-developed sense of melodrama.

The Doctor decided this was a good time to begin the interrogation of his witness. 'Romana,' he said, adopting the tones of an incisive barrister, 'when we opened the cabins aboard this vessel – what did we find?'

'Bodies. Dead bodies.'

'Could you be more specific?'

'Well, inside every cabin and cell there appeared to be something that had died ages ago.'

The Doctor nodded to the Megara. 'When we found the cabins in which their Honours were travelling, could you see what was inside?'

Romana admitted that she had had no idea who or what was travelling in the special cabins. 'It could have been any life form.'

'Did you think there was a possibility that any were still alive?'

'Yes. Of course. That is why we were so careful opening that particular cabin.'

'No further questions,' declared the Doctor. He seemed to be enjoying himself. With that, the cerebral clamp unhooked itself from Romana, who immediately put her hand to her head to check that nothing remained attached to her skull.

'The truth assessor leaves no unsightly marks on witnesses,' observed Megara One.

'Thank heavens,' said a relieved Romana, who had been afraid that she might now have a bald spot.

'The witness is excused,' said Megara Two. 'Miss Romanadvoratrelundar, you may leave the stand. But do not leave this vessel lest we should require you again.'

Back in Miss Fay's cottage, Professor Rumford was standing at the large oak table making a new version of the Doctor's machine. As she soldered a circuit, she looked up at K-9 for confirmation. 'How's that?' she asked.

'You have linked the Alpha circuit to the Sine interphase,' came the reply.

'I have?' said the Professor, in some surprise. 'Is that good?'

'Affirmative.'

'It's not as difficult as I thought, being an engineer,'

remarked the Professor gaining confidence with every application of the soldering wire. 'It's really quite simple when you know how.' Until now her experience of things mechanical had been limited to replacing the chain on her bicycle or mending a puncture in one of its tyres. Now she felt she could tackle anything. No job was too large.

'Continue,' said K-9.

The trial was proceeding apace. The Doctor was calling his second witness – Miss Vivien Fay. Miss Fay reacted with fear and anger – a startling change from the confident manner with which she had previously handled the Justice Machines.

'But I'm not a witness,' she protested.

'That's for their Honours to decide,' said the Doctor. 'It is not for you, a mere biological life form, to question the decisions of the Megara.'

'Quite right,' said Megara Two. 'Doctor, I am pleased to see that you have accepted our authority in this matter without recourse to that tiresome casuistry which only serves to delay and complicate the proceedings.'

The Doctor inclined his head. 'I bow to your Honours' vast knowledge of the Law. I call Miss Fay!'

'No,' she snapped. 'I'm not a witness. I didn't see anything. I don't know anything.'

'I call Miss Fay,' repeated the Doctor. 'Please take the stand.'

'No!'

'Once you have been called, you must appear,' pointed out Megara Two. 'It is the Law.'

But Miss Fay decided that matters had gone far enough. Those ridiculous little globes were getting above themselves. She was the Cailleach. If necessary, she would demonstrate her powers with the might of the Ogri.

'I warn you,' she said to Megara Two. 'If you persist in this nonsense, I shall be forced to set my servants on you.'

A beam of light flashed from Megara Two and irradiated the Ogri which stood beside Miss Fay. There was the sound of breaking rock, a low rumble like thunder, and in a matter of seconds the Ogri was no more than a pile of rubble and sand. Miss Fay stared aghast at the remains of her once formidable bodyguard. The speed with which its demolition had occurred had taken her breath away. She had clearly underestimated those little globes. Perhaps a more obsequious attitude to these awful machines would be advisable.

'Very well. I will take the oath,' she said demurely, proceeding to repeat the vows that Romana had taken so reluctantly.

'What are you up to?' Romana asked the Doctor meanwhile, in a whisper.

Conspiratorially, he cupped his hand over his mouth. 'I'm going to find out who she really is.'

'Will that help?'

'It might just save my life,' he replied. 'Why were the Megara and Miss Fay travelling on the same ship?'

'There might be a perfectly innocent explanation.'

The Doctor raised his eyebrows. 'Innocence doesn't seem to be a concept the Megara are familiar with. I think she was a prisoner, just like all those other poor wretches.'

Still whispering, Romana pointed out, 'If you're right and they are after Miss Fay, why don't they just arrest her?'

'They're justices – not policemen,' he replied. 'I suspect the paperwork isn't up to date. How can it be? Four thousand years have passed.'

The Megara's preliminary interrogation of Miss Fay was under way. As they burbled to each other, Romana remarked, 'It's a pity all these creatures are dead. I mean, all we need is for one of them to identify her as whatever her real name is, murderer of whoever she's killed. A description. A voice print. Anything would do.' She paused, struck by a sudden idea. 'Wait. Do you think there's anything in her cottage that still might incriminate her?'

'Possibly,' said the Doctor. 'Although the Professor and K-9 have been through her cottage with a fine-tooth comb.'

'When are they due to try and bring you back?' hissed Romana. 'They may have missed something. If I can only get through, I can check . . .'

'It's worth a try,' the Doctor whispered back, though he held little hope of any such stroke of luck. 'If you *can* get back to Earth, don't be too long. Justice Machines don't like hanging around.'

As if on cue, Megara One announced, 'We are waiting, Doctor. Are you ready to continue?'

The Doctor bowed to the silver globes. 'My apologies to your Honours. I was conferring with my associate.'

As Romana slipped away, Miss Fay immediately became suspicious. 'Where is that girl going?' she enquired loudly. 'She has no right to leave the Court without the judges' permission. I demand that she be brought back here!' And then hastily she added, 'Request. I *request*.'

'What does it matter where she goes?' observed the Doctor. 'We all know that no one can escape the Megara. Am I not right, your Honours?'

'Proceed with your questioning, Doctor,' suggested Megara Two. 'As swiftly as possible. Your execution is long overdue.'

Miss Fay signalled to the sole remaining Ogri to follow Romana. The huge stone creature lumbered away after her.

'I request that this witness be attached to the truth assessor,' said the Doctor.

'Unnecessary,' remarked Megara One.

The Doctor was taken aback. Getting Miss Fay into

a position where she could not lie was part of his strategy. If that failed, how was he going to be able to turn the tables on her? She wouldn't tell the truth unless forced to, and the truth assessor seemed the only way he could do this.

'The previous witness was attached to the assessor,' he protested vehemently. 'This one should be. Surely.'

The First Megara graciously explained the logic of their decision. 'The first witness was present when the seals to our compartment were broken. The second witness was not. Obviously, she cannot give evidence about something she has not seen. Thus, the assessor is not necessary.'

Miss Fay smiled sweetly at the Doctor, who was beginning to feel trapped. Ridiculous as these two silver globes might seem, they were extraordinarily powerful and clearly not susceptible to any appeal.

'I personally think that all witnesses should be treated the same,' he said. 'It has many advantages. Think. With everyone wearing a truth assessor, lying in court could be eliminated. Trials could be made shorter.'

'An interesting point,' agreed Megara Two. 'But irrelevant. You will proceed with your interrogation of this witness now.'

Romana had run down the corridor well ahead of the pursuant Ogri and had now reached the mark on the deck which indicated the Doctor's arrival point.

'Come on, come on, Professor,' she wished aloud. 'Switch on now!'

But in the stone circle, the Professor was having problems of her own.

'Perhaps,' she was saying to K-9, 'I ought to check the wiring again.'

The rebuilt hyperspace drive stood on the altar stone where the Professor was tinkering with its innards.

'Unnecessary,' said K-9.

'Suppose I've rigged up something wrongly?'

'You have not. I have been superintending the work.'

'Just the same,' said the Professor. 'Perhaps we ought to double-check.'

K-9 made a noise which sounded very much like electronic huffing. 'I do not make mistakes. Time is of the essence. Switch on, Professor!'

Immediately the Professor did so, a humming noise rose in the circle, followed by a flash of blue light and the appearance of a whirling vortex. Emilia was startled to see both Romana and the huge Ogri appear out of nowhere. Giddy from the transfer process, Romana quickly recovered herself and leapt to her feet, shouting, 'Quick, Professor! Run for it!'

Her warning sparked the latter into life. Fortunately, the Ogri also seemed momentarily disorientated. With

K-9 scooped up in Romana's arms, the women fled into the night.

The Doctor was beginning to despair of getting anywhere with the Megara. Maybe it was time to change tactics. Hitherto he had gone along with the silver globes. Perhaps now he ought to stop cooperating – question their authority, put them on the back foot for a change. Of course, there was one problem – how to do that and survive?

He turned to the Megara, bowed, and went on the attack. 'I submit most respectfully that your Honours are in error,' he said.

'Error? Impossible!' snapped Megara Two.

'We are programmed against the possibility of error,' declared Megara One, unwittingly echoing K-9's recent declaration. 'We are Justice Machines, containers of the Law. You are surely not suggesting that there can be errors in the Law.'

Now they began speaking together. 'Such views cannot be tolerated. The propagation thereof is punishable by death,' they stated.

The Doctor stuck his neck out and ploughed on. 'But you have rules, have you not, that this witness need not be attached to the truth assessor, because she was not present when the seals on your compartment were broken?'

'Correct,' said Megara One.

'How do you know?' demanded the Doctor. 'How can you be sure?'

'Because we did not see her when we emerged,' explained Megara Two.

'That is not proof. Because you didn't see someone is not proof that they were not there.'

'But that would imply that we were in error,' objected Megara One.

'Not necessarily. You simply didn't notice someone who was standing there.'

'It is still an error. And we are designed to be incapable of error.'

'It's only an error if you make it so,' said the Doctor magnanimously. 'I would prefer to think of it as part of a learning curve. A blank spot through which Miss Fay slipped past you.'

Megara One bleeped testily. 'But then what is to prevent her, or anyone else, from using this blank spot again?'

'Where is the blank spot?' asked Megara Two. 'We will eliminate it.'

'An excellent question,' agreed the Doctor. 'My point is that we shall never know for sure until Miss Fay is forced to wear the truth assessor and answer questions.'

'I object,' interjected Miss Fay.

'Objection overruled,' said Megara Two.

The Doctor heaved a sigh of relief: he would be able to question the Cailleach after all.

But Miss Fay wasn't finished yet. She bowed graciously to the two Megara. 'If it would simplify the proceedings, your Honours,' she said, 'I am agreeable to answering questions concerning whether I did or did not break the seal on your Honours' compartment. Attach me to your sensors, ask me that question, and I will answer truthfully.'

Professor Rumford paused for breath outside Miss Fay's cottage as Romana and K-9 caught up with her. 'It was a good idea of yours, Romana, to put out the torch,' she remarked.

'I suspected the Ogri was tracking the light,' explained Romana.

The Professor rummaged in her coat pockets for the front door key. 'I bet we've left that stone thing miles behind,' she said. 'Perhaps we've lost it for good.'

'I doubt it,' replied Romana. 'Whatever you may say about the Ogri – and I agree they're none too bright, even for stones – you have to give them ten out of ten for trying.'

Eventually the Professor unlocked the cottage door and switched on the lights. 'I would warn you that the place is in an awful mess. I turned it upside down looking for tritium crystals.'

Romana saw what she meant. The once neat cottage

looked as if a fission device had detonated close by. She hastily went round drawing curtains, in case the light attracted the Ogri.

'K-9,' she ordered, 'stay on guard. I want to know when the Ogri is approaching.'

'Affirmative, mistress,' replied the robot dog, stationing himself by the front door.

Romana turned to Emilia. 'You've been staying here a while now, Professor. You've spent time in Miss Fay's company. Is there anywhere in the house she didn't like you to go?'

The Professor gave this some thought, then shook her head. 'Vivien was always so free and easy with the place.'

Romana nodded. 'Well, is there anything she kept locked?'

Once again, the reaction was negative. Romana's quest for evidence was not going well.

Miss Fay stood with the truth assessor attached to her head.

'Are you ready, Miss Fay?' enquired Megara Two.

'Ready, your Honour,' the witness replied, affecting a look of nervousness.

'There is nothing that should concern you,' continued Megara Two. 'All you have to do is to answer my questions truthfully. Should you lie, the assessor will register the degree of untruth and react accordingly. Do you understand?'

Miss Fay nodded. She was ready for their questions.

Megara Two asked: 'Did you, or did you not, remove the seals from the official compartments in which my colleague and I were travelling?'

'I did not,' declared Miss Fay.

Megara Two checked the feedback from the truth assessor and confirmed, 'A reading of zero point 6 on the scale is registered.'

This may have signified something to the Megara, but to the Doctor it was meaningless. 'What does that indicate?' he asked.

'It is an answer within the legal definition of truth,' explained Megara Two.

'Are you sure?' asked the Doctor.

'We do not make mistakes,' reiterated Megara One.

But the Doctor was no longer prepared to accept their protestations of infallibility. 'How do you know?' he demanded. 'You've been sealed in that compartment for at least four thousand Earth years. Even the finest piece of machinery deteriorates after time. Rust. Dust. The effect of planetary magnetisation and demagnetisation over the years. All this could have affected you.'

'Nonsense,' said Megara Two. 'Our designers took into consideration all these factors.'

'So you say,' said the Doctor. 'But how would you feel, as Justice Machines, if you condemned an innocent humanoid to death simply because you'd got a piece of fluff caught in your sprocket wheels, or whatever it is you've got in those globes?'

'It would never happen,' declared Megara Two. 'Our design and construction is perfect.'

'We are a microcellular metallic organism,' explained Megara One. 'Living cells inside specially constructed globes.'

'We are, in fact, bio machines,' continued Megara Two.

'Incapable of error,' enjoined Megara One.

'Very well,' replied the Doctor. 'If you're so perfect, test yourselves. I dare you to ask Miss Fay what her real name is?'

'Irrelevant,' declared Megara Two.

'Irrational,' said Megara One.

Apparently satisfied that the Doctor's questioning of Miss Fay was at an end, Megara Two returned uncompromisingly to the original charge.

'Doctor, you admitted to breaking the seal without proper authorisation,' it announced. 'And the penalty for that offence is execution.'

The Doctor turned to Megara One. 'Have you nothing to say?' he demanded.

Clinically, his counsel replied, 'I have said everything relevant in your defence.'

'A great lawyer you turned out to be,' said the Doctor bitterly.

'You are my client. I have your interests at heart. I do not wish you to suffer unduly. I shall therefore plead with my colleague for a swift, painless death for you.'

'Your plea is granted,' said Megara Two; the Doctor suspected it was looking forward to its role as executioner.

'You see, Doctor,' said Megara One. 'Justice can be merciful.' Then, noticing Miss Fay was still wearing the truth assessor, it hovered over her. 'You may step down, Miss Fay.'

Miss Fay bowed to the Megara and left the witness stand.

Megara One advised its fellow, 'Proceed with the execution immediately.'

'Objection!' shouted the Doctor.

'To what are you objecting now?' demanded Megara Two, huffily.

'I haven't finished presenting my case,' insisted the Doctor. 'I have another witness I want to call.'

Megara One was clearly confused by the new development. 'But there are no other witnesses here,' it said.

'You're wrong, your Honour,' announced the Doctor. 'There is another witness I can call.'

'Who?' demanded Megara One.

The Doctor grinned. 'You.'

Chapter X

Execution

Drawers had been opened, and their contents piled on the floor. Books and papers were spread everywhere in the cottage. The whole place looked to be in the throes of a raid by the Gestapo.

The Professor looked round the sitting room sadly, remembering how tidy Miss Fay had always been. Everything in its place, and a place for everything. Regardless, her erstwhile companion had never criticised the Professor's predilection for spreading out her work on every available surface and leaving it there until required for later consultation. Only in small, subtle ways had she conveyed her irritation at finding, say, three volumes of *Heywood's West Country Worthies* open on the kitchen table, the fourth volume in the pantry on top of the bread bin, and volume five in the wrong place on the bookshelf. Mostly she had simply professed amazement that her lodger knew where everything was and could usually lay her hands on it at a moment's notice.

'In lots of ways,' remarked the Professor, wistfully,

'Vivien and I got on very well. She has many admirable qualities.'

'I assume you aren't including her attachment to the Ogri among them,' replied Romana drily. She had little time for sentiment.

'It still defeats me how an intelligent woman could have anything in common with those homicidal chunks of granite,' said the Professor. She looked around. 'This is hopeless. We don't even know what we're looking for. For all we know we've already seen it. Or maybe it isn't here at all.' She turned to K-9, who was investigating the interior of a cupboard. 'Have you found anything, little fellow?'

'Negative, Professor,' he replied.

Romana, who had been studying a shelf of cookery books, suddenly declared, 'Citric acid!'

'What?' demanded the Professor.

'It's found in the juice of citrus fruit.'

'I know what citric acid is, girl,' Emilia replied testily. 'What I don't see is what it's got to do with investigating Vivien Fay.'

'She doesn't seem to have liked the stuff,' said Romana. 'She's crossed it out of any recipes.'

'She once told me she was allergic to lemons,' replied the Professor, still totally mystified. 'Any citrus fruit, come to that. Oranges. Grapefruit. Whatever. But I still don't see what you're getting at.'

Romana closed an ancient volume of recipes with a

triumphant flourish. 'Ever wondered why the Ogri don't attack her? Why should she be safe when we're not?'

Emilia sniffed. 'I presume they don't fancy her blood.'

'Precisely,' agreed Romana. 'Which must mean that Vivien Fay's metabolism is totally different from Earth-born humans. K-9!' At her call, the automaton emerged from yet another cupboard. 'If Miss Fay has an alien physiology with a severe citrus allergy and blood that would poison an Ogri, which planets is she most likely to come from?'

'Checking memory banks, mistress,' replied the robot, his circuits buzzing like a hive of metal bees.

The Justice Machines were attempting to dissuade the Doctor from calling one of them as witness in his trial.

'We cannot be called upon to give evidence,' protested Megara One.

'Why not?' demanded the Doctor.

'Because we are Justice Machines,' both Megara replied. 'We are judge, jury and executioner. We are not witnesses.'

'Yes, but why not?' repeated the Doctor.

'It would be undignified,' complained Megara Two.

'And unseemly,' agreed its colleague. 'We are not programmed to give evidence. Our creators never even considered the possibility.'

'The question as I see it,' said the Doctor, 'is whether it is against the Law for me to put my own counsel on the stand. Surely there's no law that says I can't do that . . .' He paused, waiting for a reply, and waited and waited. 'Well? Is there?' he asked.

Finally Megara Two announced its ruling: 'According to our databanks, the Law does not actually specify that the accused may not call his own counsel, but—'

'I call the Megara,' interjected the Doctor.

'But,' continued Megara Two, "it is most unorthodox. And indeed may be grounds for a charge of contempt of court at a later date.'

The Doctor ignored the implied threat and proceeded without further ado. He said to the Megara, 'I shall, of course, dispense with the oath, your Honour.'

Both Megara were in no doubt about that. 'An oath is not necessary,' they said. 'The Megara cannot lie.'

'I accept that,' declared the Doctor. 'My first question to my counsel is – why were you sealed into your compartment?'

'Because we are Justice Machines travelling on judicial business.'

'But why are the compartments sealed?'

'To prevent any contamination by outside influences before a trial. Our creators believed that justice could only be seen to be done if the machines involved were inviolate, uninfluenced in any way by any participants in the trial. And so, they advocated this form of judicial antisepsis – on pain of instant execution if the machines were impeded or obstructed in any way.'

'Surely that is precisely what the Doctor has been doing,' insisted Miss Fay. 'He should be executed immediately.'

'Execution is our decision,' said Megara Two. 'Not yours. If you interfere any further in this case, you will be held in contempt of court.'

This had a quietening effect on Miss Fay.

'Which planet were you travelling to?' asked the Doctor, still following his line of enquiry.

'Diplos,' came the reply. 'A small G-class planet in Tau Ceti.'

The Doctor considered this, then asked, 'For what purpose?'

'In order to try a female humanoid criminal.'

A smile broke across the Doctor's face. Who else could that be?

By coincidence, K-9 had just reached a similar conclusion about Miss Fay's origins. A thorough search of his databanks suggested unequivocally that she came from a small G-class planet in Tau Ceti.

'That's encouraging,' suggested Professor Rumford.

'There are 750 G-class planets in that particular system,' K-9 qualified.

'But only two of them are capable of supporting humanoid life,' pointed out Romana, always delighted to put one over on K-9. 'Besides,' she added, 'the planet Ogros, home of the Ogri, is in the same solar system.'

The Professor was convinced. 'Sounds pretty conclusive to me,' she said. 'But does it help us?'

'Know your enemy,' said Romana. 'And you'll know when to duck. At least, that's what the Doctor says.'

'Talking of enemies,' enquired the Professor, 'we seem to have ignored ours for some time. Do we know where our wandering lump of granite is right now?'

K-9's sensors whirred, and he suddenly pronounced, 'Ogri approaching.'

The Professor closed her eyes and sighed. 'So we didn't lose it after all.'

'How close is it?' asked Romana.

K-9's reply was lost in a sudden cacophony, as the front door of the cottage disintegrated in a shower of splinters and stone chippings to reveal the huge stone creature blocking the entrance.

Without hesitation, Romana scooped up K-9 and then she and the Professor fled into the kitchen and out through the back door. As they ran across the moor towards the circle, they could hear the Ogri practically demolishing the cottage in pursuit of them. It sounded like a sixty-tonne tank on manoeuvres.

'I do hope Vivien is insured,' panted the Professor, bringing up the rear.

At his trial, the Doctor was trying to ascertain a few facts about the Megara's mysterious prisoner.

'Of what crime is the female humanoid accused?' he enquired.

'Murder,' replied Megara One. 'Plus the theft and misuse of the Great Seal of Diplos.'

'I'm surprised Diplos had a Great Seal,' observed the Doctor. He knew that the planets of Tau Ceti were mostly volcanic hellholes, circling too closely to their various suns to sustain intelligent life.

Megara One explained, 'There is reason to believe that it was left behind by a craft of reptilian life forms on their way to a destination somewhere in the Magellanic Cloud. They arrived, but their Great Seal did not. For some reason it remained behind on Diplos, and came into the possession of the natives, who discovered its power.'

'Power? To do what?'

'The power to transmute, transform—'

'And to establish hyperspatial and temporal coordinates,' declared the Doctor, completing Megara One's sentence. 'Of course! I knew she had to have something like that. Otherwise how could she get out of a prison ship?'

But Megara Two was impatient with the constant delays in the proceedings. The Megara are famous for the speed and correctness of their verdicts, and here was this convicted breaker of seals doing his best to delay things even more.

'None of that is relevant,' declared Megara Two. 'Nor are these matters which ought to be discussed prior to the trial of Cessair of Diplos . . .'

'So that's her real name,' exclaimed the Doctor. 'Thank you.'

'As I was saying,' went on Megara Two, 'these are not matters which we ought to discuss with a male humanoid convicted of a capital crime and awaiting execution.'

'Hear, hear,' applauded Miss Fay.

'Silence! Or I shall be forced to order the executions of all humanoid life forms on this vessel!' Megara Two was rapidly losing its temper. What had begun as a relatively straightforward case was in danger of descending into farce.

'Do you have her description?' asked the Doctor. 'Any photographic likeness? Or genome analysis?'

'We do not,' confessed Megara One.

'Then how were you planning to identify her?' enquired the Doctor.

Megara One explained that on their arrival at their destination, which was the prison planet Heliades, they were to have been met by an officer of the court. He could identify Cessair of Diplos, having arrested her on previous occasions. Because so many of the species in the galaxy possessed the ability to mutate or otherwise change their appearance, personal identification was therefore often the most reliable.

'Was there any guarantee,' asked the Doctor, 'that this one official who could make the identification would still be alive, *compos mentis*, and ready to identify her after four thousand years?'

'None,' admitted Megara One.

Greatly encouraged by this piece of news, Miss Fay immediately demanded, 'When is the accused to be executed? His termination was promised by your Honours some time ago. I await it with eager anticipation.'

'Aren't you being a bit ghoulish?' complained the Doctor. 'I'm sure their Honours will get around to me in their own good time. Meanwhile perhaps they ought to be sorting out your identity.'

'This female humanoid's identity is not in question,' stated Megara Two.

'It should be,' declared the Doctor. 'Because she is in fact Cessair of Diplos, wanted for murder and theft. There has been no interrogation of her. You have simply accepted her word without question.'

But the Megara weren't interested. 'We have performed the duties required of us by Law,' said Megara Two.

'Your prevarications have been tolerated for long enough,' Megara One added. 'Our only remaining task is to carry out your painless execution.'

But the Doctor wasn't ready to give up yet. 'Ask yourselves,' he pleaded, 'for what other reason could

Vivien Fay be in hyperspace? If she isn't Cessair of Diplos, who else can she be?'

'That is not our concern. Such speculation is pointless. Besides, Miss Fay's name does not appear on the vessel's manifest.'

'Of course, it doesn't,' cried the Doctor in increasing frustration. 'Because she's down under her real name, Cessair of Diplos.'

'You have produced no evidence to lead to such a presumption,' pointed out Megara Two.

His colleague added, 'The Law cannot operate on unsubstantiated accusations. Only on hard evidence. And you have none. As your defence counsel I regret that fact, naturally, but the Law must take its course.'

Megara One clamped the truth assessor onto the Doctor's head. 'I assure you this will not hurt,' it said. 'Prepare yourself for death.'

'About time, too,' declared Miss Fay, moving closer to the Doctor. 'All you Megara ever seem to do is talk. Kill him!'

'One question,' demanded the Doctor as the assessor's probes slid into his skull. 'Do you always execute your own clients?'

'Only when they are guilty,' replied Megara One. 'If there is any doubt we do not.'

'It certainly adds a new dimension to the role of defence counsel . . .'

The two Megara hovered closer to the Doctor, ready to commit the act.

'Wait a minute. Wait a minute,' said the Doctor. 'Not so fast. Aren't you going to offer me a last toffee apple? A hearty breakfast? No?'

'No,' confirmed Megara One.

As the air around the two silver globes began to crackle with electricity, the Doctor leaped at Miss Fay, seizing her in his arms. There was a blinding flash of light, and both Miss Fay and the Doctor were irradiated. Together they collapsed in a heap on the floor . . .

Chapter XI

A Meeting on the Moor

Having been set down by Romana at the stone circle, K-9 was finding it increasingly difficult to hold back the Ogri. As it tried repeatedly to breach K-9's force field, the automaton trundled backwards a short distance.

'Cannot restrain aggressor much longer,' he squeaked.

Romana moved to take up position in front of the hyperspace drive. 'Now,' she called to the Professor. 'Switch on!'

She arrived in hyperspace with the usual bone-jarring thump. Steeling herself, she sat up dizzily on the deck of the vessel, then paused for a second to catch her breath and get her bearings. She then ran towards where the Megara were holding their impromptu court – and gasped at the sight of the two silver globes hovering above the recumbent bodies of the Doctor and Miss Fay. The Megara were buzzing at each other like a couple of angry wasps.

'You've killed them both!' Romana cried. 'A fine pair of Justice Machines you turned out to be!'

'The execution charge was administered to both humanoids in error,' one Megara protested. 'We could not have anticipated a murder attempt.'

'We should have done,' admitted Megara One. 'There can be no excuses. We are in error.'

'We cannot be. It is impossible.'

'If we are not in error, then why are two humanoids lying here?' demanded Megara One. 'We have failed in our duty to the Law.'

The debate might have gone on for ever, were it not for the fact that the Doctor was reviving. He rose to his feet on wobbly legs, staggering about like a drunkard. The Megara immediately buzzed around him.

'Never mind me,' he told them. 'It's Miss Fay you ought to worry about.'

The woman was still unconscious.

Megara Two was indignant at the Doctor's actions. 'Why did you try to involve Miss Fay in your execution?' it demanded. 'You could have killed her.'

'You were the ones doing the killing,' pointed out the Doctor. 'I was the one being executed. Remember? Incidentally, why did you stop?'

'We were forced to abort your execution, since the charge intended to kill you would have killed her as well – and we have no legal authority to kill her.'

The Doctor felt Miss Fay's pulse, lifted her eyelids and made sure she was still breathing. 'Well, you're lucky,' he declared. 'She's still alive.'

'Good,' said Megara Two. 'Then we can proceed with your execution as planned. Without the involvement of Miss Fay.'

'But who knows what damage you've done to this poor woman?' the Doctor speculated. 'The humanoid brain is a very delicate organ, you know. But of course you wouldn't know, seeing that you're machines.'

The two Megara indulged in a bout of mutual buzzing before turning to the Doctor again. 'What do you suggest?' asked Megara One, tentatively.

'Put the truth assessor on her. That should tell you immediately if there is any brain damage.'

'An excellent idea,' agreed Megara One. 'Please be patient while we delay your execution for a further short period.'

'Take your time,' said the Doctor graciously. 'No need to hurry on my account. Better to make sure that all's well than find out later that you've fried her brain to a crisp. Think of the suits for damages you could face . . .' He watched as the metal cap of the truth assessor attached itself to Miss Fay's skull. 'Check her memory cells first,' he advised. 'Ask her to identify herself. Find out which planet she comes from.'

But Megara One resented the Doctor's interference. 'We are quite capable of conducting our own investigation,' it snapped. 'You would be better employed preparing yourself for dissolution.'

But by this time Megara Two was indeed linked to

the truth assessor. There was a flash, and the crackle of static electricity, which made Miss Fay's legs twitch.

After a long pause, Megara Two announced, 'I am reaching into the humanoid's memories. Deep into her memory . . .' The Justice Machine gave an urgent flashing of sparks. 'This humanoid is *not* Vivien Fay. She is Cessair of Diplos. Guilty of the theft and misuse of the Great Seal of Diplos . . .'

'No! Really?' the Doctor exclaimed with pantomime shock.

The revelations did not end there. It also emerged that she had removed three silicon-based life forms from the planet Ogros, in contravention of Article 7594 of the Galactic Charter, and furthermore had forced them to do her bidding. To wit, the killing of countless humanoids on planet Earth.

'Well, well,' murmured the Doctor smugly. 'We live and learn. Just shows you can't trust anyone these days. Who'd have thought Miss Fay would turn out to be Cessair of Diplos, master criminal and all-round bad egg? I hate to say "I told you so", but I told you so. I expect she thought it was her lucky day when Romana and I came along. Two clever deckhands to help her pilot this ship.'

On the floor, Miss Fay had begun to stir. She groaned, rubbed her aching head, and then tried and failed to struggle to her feet. The Doctor put an arm around her and helped her to stand. 'Being executed takes it out of you, doesn't it?' he said sympathetically.

But Vivien Fay was beyond sympathy and was still trying to gather her wits together. She was aware that something momentous had happened. But what?

'What have you done to me?' she gasped.

'I saved you from execution,' explained the Doctor. 'No, don't thank me. It was my pleasure.'

'Your attempt to make this creature share in your punishment was intended to trick us into invading the memory of this female humanoid,' complained Megara Two.

'And to prevent your Honours from making a terrible error of judgement,' pointed out the Doctor. 'For which I ought to be rewarded. My death sentence should be rescinded.'

'If we started rescinding death sentences,' pointed out Megara Two, 'we should be circuit-deep in criminals in no time. Request denied.'

The Doctor pulled a face. 'There's gratitude for you. Tell me, what happens to Justice Machines that make mistakes?'

'They are disassembled.'

'So, it's only thanks to me that you're not in pieces in a box somewhere.'

'Gratitude,' pointed out Megara One, 'is not one of our functions. Indeed, nothing can sway us once decisions have been made according to the Law. Our designers strove for clarity, inflexibility and infallibility when they created us.'

'Well, they certainly slipped up there,' observed the Doctor. 'You're about as infallible as a couple of headless chickens.'

At that point Romana noticed the presence of an Ogri looming behind her. Clearly K-9's barrier had been breached, and the Professor must have beamed it through – perhaps by accident but more credibly by design, to save K-9 and herself. The creature paused for a moment, as if awaiting orders from Miss Fay, who was quick to oblige.

'Help me, Ogri! Help me now!'

Megara One intervened before the creature could move. 'Stop!' it commanded. 'We are the Megara. None may threaten the Megara on pain of immediate disintegration. Ogri, do not move!'

Apparently recognising the threat as a genuine one, the Ogri came to an abrupt halt, and remained still.

Megara Two, meanwhile, had busied itself with the case of the duplicitous female humanoid. Based on the contents of her memory, the machine had discovered irrefutable evidence of a litany of crimes and misdemeanours, of which two came squarely under the jurisdiction of Machine Law.

'Cessair of Diplos,' it began, 'you have been tried and found guilty of the following charges: impersonating a religious personage, to wit, a Celtic goddess, for which the penalty is imprisonment for one thousand, five hundred years; theft of the Great Seal of Diplos, for which the penalty is perpetual imprisonment. The sentences to run consecutively. Have you anything to say before sentence is passed?

'Yes,' screamed Cessair of Diplos, pointing to the Doctor. 'Kill him first!'

A cold, early morning light was creeping rapidly across the moor. Huddled in her duffel coat, Professor Rumford had not quite given up hope of seeing the Doctor and Romana again. When the Ogri had charged into the hyperspace beam and disappeared into thin air, she had hotly proposed that K-9 beam her through after it, if only to even up the odds against the other two. But the little dog had advised against precipitate action. They simply didn't know what awaited them in hyperspace, he pointed out. (Privately, he had calculated that the sudden arrival of a sixty-year-old academic could easily prove more of a hindrance than a help to the Doctor and Romana.)

Yet Emilia had insisted that, if the other two didn't appear shortly, she was going in herself. They were still arguing about this when, in a sudden flash of bright light, the Doctor, Romana, Miss Fay and the two Megara materialised, apparently out of nowhere.

The Professor eyed the Megara uncertainly as they came close to her. They reminded her of over-large Christmas tree decorations, except that there was a crackle of static electricity about them which she found unsettling.

'What are they?' she asked.

'Justice Machines,' explained the Doctor, sotto voce. 'Treat them with the greatest respect. They're very touchy and extremely dangerous. And when it comes to them carrying out a judicial sentence, I'd stand well back if I were you.'

'What sentence?' asked the Professor.

'Wait and see.'

'*You* wait.' Romana tugged at the Doctor's coat sleeve. 'What about the third segment? Those weak readings the Tracer detected . . .'

'The segment was on the move.' The Doctor looked at Miss Fay. 'Crossing between here and hyperspace . . .'

At his words, Miss Fay's fingers strayed unconsciously to the large pendant she wore. As she did so, the jewel seemed almost to glow.

The Doctor beamed as he turned to the Megara. 'Excuse me, your Honours. I believe this belongs to me!' He leapt forward and snatched the pendant from around Miss Fay's neck, hastily stepping back when the Megara began buzzing loudly.

'Give that back!' Miss Fay demanded, making no attempt to hide her terror at being separated from the necklace.

'Not a chance,' replied the Doctor.

Romana stared. '*That's* the segment!'

'Segment of what?' said the Professor baffled.

'Oh, just another stone of uncertain origin,' the

Doctor said airily. 'Stolen, of course. Romana and I have been looking for it for some time.'

'We're returning it to the rightful owner,' Romana assured her.

'I am the rightful owner!' hissed Vivien Fay.

'Finders, keepers? Not on this occasion,' said the Doctor. 'I daresay this has come in handy over the years, with its powers of transmutation and telepathy. It's allowed you to exert low-level control over many of the local life forms. You've even had the birds at your beck and call. Perhaps you think you can use it to escape imprisonment, hmm . . . ?'

'Your Honours,' Miss Fay begged, 'that is not his property to take!'

'Your accoutrements are of no interest to the Megara. We are Justice Machines,' they intoned, apparently unconcerned about the pendant, 'appointed by the Galactic Grand Council – Legal Division – to execute the Law. We have passed sentence on Cessair of Diplos and this we now carry out.'

A dual beam of light shot from the two spheres and converged on their prisoner. The Professor and Romana watched in appalled fascination, as Vivien Fay was first turned into a stone statue, and then gradually encased in a huge granite block. She became a monolith, fifteen or more feet high. The last words she spoke were, 'You can't do this to me . . . !'

Then there was silence.

'Poor Vivien,' said the Professor sadly. 'Is she dead?'

'Who knows,' replied the Doctor. 'I've heard the Diploids don't die easily. But could anyone survive inside a stone?'

'From what I've learnt of Vivien,' ventured the Professor, wagging a finger at the new monolith, 'she'll be out of there in three or four hundred years and up to her old tricks again.'

'You are mistaken,' declared Megara Two. 'Escape from judicial entombment is impossible. She will suffer her sentence according to the Law. Which brings us to some unfinished legal business, Doctor – your execution.'

'Oh, I don't think we'll bother with that,' replied the Doctor. He pointed the pendant at the Megara. There was a blinding flash, and the two silver globes vanished.

'Safe journey,' he called.

The Professor's eyes widened. 'That pendant has some very interesting properties.'

'Scintillating!' the Doctor agreed cheerily. 'Don't worry, we'll keep it safe.

'What's to stop the Megara coming straight back?' asked Romana. 'They don't need crystalline help to travel between here and hyperspace.'

'They're on their way to Diplos,' the Doctor replied. 'Not the most interesting planet in the galaxy, I grant you, though I'm sure they'll find lots of fascinating things to do when they get there. They'll need to make a full report to the authorities. Which should take them a long, long time. You see, I took the liberty of pre-setting their ship's flight controls before we all popped down here. If nothing else, it should give me a couple of thousand years' grace before they manage to get back here. Now then, we've got a quest to be getting on with. Time to go, Romana. Back to the TARDIS.' He turned to his other companion. 'Come along, K-9. Don't dilly-dally.'

'I never do,' the automaton complained.

And so, they set off across the moor, in the direction of the TARDIS.

As the Professor plodded along beside them, she was struck with a disturbing thought. 'What about Vivien?' she asked. 'We can't just leave her back there in the circle.'

'Yes, we can,' the Doctor insisted. 'She's been concealing herself in this area for so long, it seems fitting she remains, don't you think? And she'll be quite safe. Well, apart from the odd bit of graffiti.'

All the same, the Professor wasn't happy about leaving her one-time assistant encased in stone. Perhaps if she took a hammer and chisel to it, she could cut her free. But then what? Vivien Fay's past history suggested that gratitude didn't loom large in her lexicon. Anyway, perhaps she could visit regularly and talk to Vivien. Yes, that would probably be safer. The locals already thought of her as that mad professor, so talking to a stone wouldn't alarm them, particularly since it couldn't answer back.

'Wait!' the Professor cried, aghast. 'You know what this means, don't you? The Nine Travellers will have to be surveyed again. Now, there's only seven of them – including one that's brand new! That'll put the cat amongst the pigeons.'

'Won't it, though! You could write a monograph about it,' the Doctor suggested.

On reflection, the idea appealed to the Professor. Such a monograph would make her pet *bête noir*, Hugh Morgan, look like a complete idiot who couldn't count. Mislaying two standing stones was not the sort of behaviour expected of a professor of megalithic archaeology.

'Will you tell the truth about what really happened in your monograph?' asked Romana.

'Of course, not,' declared the Professor. 'I do have my academic reputation to consider. How would I explain you two? Not to mention K-9. On the other hand, where am I to say Vivien's gone? How am I to explain the damage to her cottage? The local police will certainly demand some sort of statement, not to mention the insurance companies and solicitors.'

'Put it all down to earth tremors,' suggested the Doctor.

'They won't believe that, man!'

'Then keep saying it. People will believe almost anything if you say it often enough.'

'You might have something there. Vivien used to say that was the whole basis of modern politics.' Emilia sighed wistfully at the memory.

The Doctor unlocked the door of the TARDIS. The time had come for farewells, which he always thought best left to other people. Romana gave the Professor a kiss on the cheek, an Earth custom she had learnt from the TARDIS databanks, and the older woman responded with a hearty embrace. K-9 followed his mistress into the blue police box, and the Doctor paused merely to wave at the Professor before shutting the door behind him.

Emilia was just wondering where on earth they thought they were going, when there was a curious cranking sound – and the box promptly dematerialised. She rubbed her eyes and tilted her head. Was it a trick of the light? No! On stepping forward, she found she could walk right cross the square of flattened grass where the box had stood.

'Whatever the Doctor may say,' she muttered to herself, 'I'm *never* going to be able to explain that.' And then, after waiting ten minutes or so in case her strange new friends came back, she gathered herself together and made her way back to the cottage. She was going to miss everyone. It was just her now. Her and her memories.

She began to think a little harder about that monograph . . .

Once the TARDIS was on its way, spinning through space and time, Romana asked the Doctor, 'Is the Earth always like that?'

'Oh, no,' he replied. 'Sometimes things can get quite exciting.'

He took the pendant he had snatched from Vivien Fay, and laid it on the control console. Then he touched it with the Tracer wand, and together they watched it transform into a familiarly shaped chunk of gleaming crystal.

Thinking about the two segments they had already collected, he said, 'I hope you're going to demonstrate your knack with jiggling the pieces again.'

She smiled. 'Would you like me to show you how it's done, Doctor?'

'What?' came the airy reply. 'No, no, I'll leave that sort of frippery to you. K-9 and I have far more important things to do.' And then, reaching for the chessboard he kept in a nearby locker, he enquired, 'Black or white, old chap?'

Afterword

Michael Stevens

The Stones of Blood is one of my favourite *Doctor Who* TV serials – I was captivated by it as a young TV viewer in 1978. I also loved Terrance Dicks's Target novelisation, yet I was aware that it was on the 'slim' side in comparison with others in the range. In my commissioning role for BBC Audio, I realised that an adaptation by David Fisher could give us more background for the story, both in terms of character (the adorable Professor Rumford, the longevous Vivien Fay, the wretched De Vries and his acolyte with their Plymouth bolthole) and setting (the location of the Nine Travellers stone circle is unspecified on-screen; I was curious whether David had intended it to be Cornwall, where it has several likely real-life counterparts).

David responded enthusiastically to my letter, and we had a couple of phone calls to discuss approach and word count. I provided camera scripts of the TV episodes, and some months later an A4 manuscript, several inches thick, arrived at the BBC Audio office, along with an electronic version. Then I had the singular pleasure of reading a brand-new novelisation of *The Stones of Blood*.

David wrote superbly; his narrative was witty and erudite, and his characterisations were pithy and true to the live-action version. He was kind enough to take on board, along with some standard desk edits, a few suggested embellishments and clarifications of purpose, plus some advisory notes on accepted *Doctor Who* lore. In very little time we arrived at the version that was recorded in Bath by Susan Engel (who had played Vivien Fay in the TV version), for release by BBC Audio.

In 2011, writing copy for the CD inlay, David noted:

> The story of *The Stones of Blood* grew out of a long fascination with stone circles, henges and the like. This began many years ago, when I was filming in the Western Isles and visited Calinish on the Isle of Harris, where there is a circle of huge stones which were erected god-knows-when. They are simply a group of either unshaped, or very crudely shaped, stones stood on end and positioned to some plan known only to the original builders. They are incredibly beautiful in that stark, bleak landscape. You immediately ask yourself: why are they placed so precisely there? How did a relatively small population manage to achieve such a feat of engineering?

From there I became interested in other ancient monuments, like Stonehenge, Avebury, Carnac in Brittany – not forgetting the wood henge discovered a few years ago at low tide near Holme-next-the-Sea in Norfolk. They are all different and all equally mysterious. Were they astronomical observatories, giant stone calendars, stone age cathedrals, or simple places where tribes got together for a knees-up and probably a little human sacrifice?

Unfortunately, these early builders did not leave behind any written records; they never got around to inventing writing. Oh, to have a do-it-yourself guide to the Stonehengers' afterlife, something along the lines of the *Egyptian Book of the Dead*.

The Stones of Blood was my first *Doctor Who* script, and in retrospect was a very happy and relatively painless experience. Partly, I think this was because so many of the characters came with their right names attached. There is nothing worse than starting a script with a cast of characters who don't know their proper names. Is George the right name for your hero, or is he really a Kevin or a Clive? Female characters can be equally infuriating. That is why I was grateful that Professor Rumford immediately answered to her name (though truth to tell, I stole it for her from the late Kurt Vonnegut). De Vries seemed the ideal name for a dodgy little man with a wispy Van Dyke beard and a penchant for dressing up as a Druid. Vivien(ne)

Fay was Arthurian, of course. The Ogri were Latinised Ogres. The Justice Machines, the Megara, were based on the Greek Furies and ought to have been female. But they were machines, after all, and I thought that sexualising them would create unnecessary complications. Fortunately they arrived more or less word and tone perfect – though their precise appearance, a series of flashing lights in the programme (silver globes in the book) was the result of a couple of lengthy alcoholic discussions with producer Graham Williams and script editor Tony Read.

Sometimes the whole process felt positively mediaeval, as if we were trying to calculate the number of angels that could dance on the head of a pin. I think that particular praise is due to Tom Baker and Mary Tamm, who in studio had to play several long scenes with blank spaces where the Megara were supposed to be (the Justice Machines being added electronically after the shooting was complete).

Given all the things that can go wrong between the original storyline and the final programme, I am extremely grateful that everything worked out so well in *The Stones of Blood*.

I feel a similar gratitude toward David Fisher for his gusto, professionalism and hard work; my admiration for him only grew during the production of his audiobook novelisations for *The Stones of Blood* and its follow-up, *The Androids of Tara*. I know David was glad of the opportunity to revisit his scripts in this way and I'm sure that, were he alive today, he would be delighted to now see them both in print.